Critical Corner

A Thomas Ballard Mystery

D.G. Stern

NEPTUNE PRESS

NEPTUNE PRESS

WWW.NEPTUNEPRESS.ORG

Printed in the U.S.A.

Publisher's Cataloging-In-Publication Data
(Prepared by The Donohue Group, Inc.)

Names: Stern, D. G., author.
Title: Critical corner / D.G. Stern.
Description: [Orlando, Florida] : Neptune Press, [2020] | Series: A Thomas Ballard mystery
Identifiers: ISBN 9781732455139
Subjects: LCSH: Racetracks (Automobile racing)--Florida--Fiction. | Sheriffs--Florida--Fiction. | Murder--Florida--Fiction. | LCGFT: Detective and mystery fiction.
Classification: LCC PS3619.T477 C75 2020 | DDC 813/.6--dc23

What they are saying about the Thomas Ballard mysteries

Stabbing Along the Straightaway

"D.G. captured every bit of the vintage world of racing world. It's a vivid picture with believable personalities and great cars, and one "who dun it" that will keep you guessing to the very end." —Jeanette Veitenheimer Lime Rock Park Historic Festival Executive Administrator

"You have a great understanding of the characters that have passion for the sport and the cars that they race. I enjoyed the book immensely. Great story." —Stephen Page Founder, Chairman and CEO Vintage Racing League

"Stern's sense of dialog and breezy style as well as his occasional spot on observations of the vintage racing scene make for a tough book to put down." —Vintage Sports Car

Chaos at the Concours

"Well-conceived and written. The Bentley Gang were in fine form. Many, many thanks for sharing your passion for all that is "collector cars" with me." —Stephen J. L. Page, Founder & CEO, Racing and Cars

"D. G. Stern masterfully shares with the reader the complicated inner workings of Ballard's thinking, revealing how he determined the motives for the murders and the evidence that led to a conclusion of what happened. It is obvious that Stern is a lover of vintage vehicles; he even has Ballard often residing in a vintage 1955 Airstream Flying Cloud travel trailer. Chaos at

the Concours is fast-paced, exciting, and full of D. G. Stern's red herrings. If you like murder mysteries, you will appreciate Stern's work." —AuthorsReading.com

"Stern's breezy and almost (but not quite) glib style is simply great fun and we recommend this one to any and all looking for a light novel with a motoring background to the story. It is assuredly a keeper." —Vintage Sports Car

2018 First Place Books, Fiction
America Auto Racing Writers and Broadcasters Association, Inc.

Panic in the Pits

"Let's cut right to the chase, Stern's third Thomas Ballard novel, Panic in the Pits, is even better than his first two-and we loved the first two." —Vintage Sports Car

2019 Second Place Books
America Auto Racing Writers and Broadcasters Association, Inc.

To finish first, you must first finish.
— Juan Manuel Fangio—

CHAPTER ONE

Living in Central Florida has a lot of advantages: the weather is picture perfect, except during hurricane season when you run a risk of losing your roof, or during the summer when the heat index can exceed 100 degrees, or during the winter when the temperature can go from 80 degrees to 40 degrees and then back to 80 degrees-in one day.

On the plus side, motorsports abound: four wheel, two wheel, no wheel; on dirt, asphalt or water. This is especially important if you make your living, such as it is, as an automotive (including motorcycles and speed boats) journalist. I can drive from our house in Orlando about an hour easterly on I-4 and be at the iconic Daytona Speedway for early morning practice; then drift into town for the Bike Week assemblage featuring thousands of *bikers and their chicks*; then travel down I-95 about one-half hour and arrive at the old school New Smyrna oval for morning modified qualifying; then rumble up Route 44 to Tavares and see the first heat of the classic speed boat race; then scoot up to Gainesville Raceway and view NHRA machines speed down the ¼ mile drag strip. All this before happy hour. And I haven't included our local road course, Citrus Grove, where Formula One racers will be gathering in six weeks for about the coolest event-ever. The F-1 promoters recently realized what Disney and Universal have known for decades. Central Florida is the country's entertainment hub and with the construction of Citrus Grove, we now have a world class track.

I might add that I am also an Orange County (Orlando area) special deputy sheriff. I would like to think the special has something to do with my extraordinary talents as a sleuth, but I am assured by the Sheriff, who happens to be a lifelong friend, that it simply was a way for him to give me a shiny badge, although I think I have made a major contribution to solving several recent murders. Sheriff McCarthy probably would agree, but reluctantly. So would Orange County Chief Detective Olivia Nederfield with whom I have been sharing my time exclusively for over a year. I guess we are kind of engaged.

The thought of a world class automotive extravaganza taking place only twenty minutes from one's house is exciting to the journalist in me; however the logistics are a nightmare. Security and transportation are among the major headaches facing the organizers, which really mean facing the Orange County Sheriff's Department. At least we don't have to worry about concessions and the competition itself, which will include scores of races, practice and qualifying sessions for not only F-1 participants, but also the new Formula E class, like in electric, and vintage pre-1960 single-seat cars.

Sheriff Josh McCarthy is going to make me pay for my shiny badge. I have been assigned the task of checking the bona fides of the media. Since the event will be drawing folks from all over the globe, my job is rather complicated. I have only five hundred passes available, actually four hundred ninety nine since the first press credential I approved was, of course, my own. Rank has its privileges.

I never imagined the sheer volume of applications-over five thousand, which the facility, despite being state-of-the-art, cannot absorb. Both print and photo journalists are going to have to pool material. I have been sorting through requests, with pictures, resumes and even samples of previous work, for over a month. It's a lose/lose because if I reject someone, they will say that I am somehow biased because of my "day job". Even though I sign each acceptance or rejection *Thomas Ballard, Deputy Sheriff, Media Credential Supervisor,* since I have garnered somewhat of a world-wide reputation, I can't really hide. Maybe I should use a different name, like T. Calvin Ballard, which is actually my real name. I am not a big fan of my middle name, which I was given because my mother's favorite uncle was named Calvin, undoubtedly after a former president. I will muddle on.

Olivia has a tougher job-making sure all the dignitaries are safe and sound. Not only does she have to interact with the law enforcement, but also with the personal private security details many of the visiting big shots will demand. We all have to address the issue of weapon possession, which is serious and very touchy.

At an inter-departmental meeting with the state police, Florida attorney general's office and several representatives of Uncle Sam, the discussion gets very heated. "Let's break this down to the lowest common denominator. We need to identify who falls into which category."

"Spoken like a true journalist. The lowest common denominator part I mean." Sheriff McCarthy gets a chuckle from the assembled. I do not take his remark personally because although it is at my expense, his comment is intended to get everyone to lighten up.

"Deputy Ballard is right. Those who are entitled to our protection are easy to identify. I just hope the list from the White House is short and that we get it soon. We can assure you that there will be no firearms except for agents. No exceptions." Donald Driver, a senior member of the Secret Service, with whom we have worked before, says. "In order to make Sheriff McCarthy's job a little easier, we can have agents in the field as well as with the individual who is being guarded."

"I think we will need all the help we can get. I have been assured by several county Sheriffs that additional personnel will be made available," Josh responds.

"I would love the extra manpower." Detective Nederfield rises to address the group. Her use of the word *manpower* is a little ironic considering she is a drop dead, beautiful, 6'2" blonde who is considered one of the best markspersons in Florida. "Let me know how many agents you can spare and I will get them integrated into race families. Thomas, at least ten agents will have to have media credentials so that they can move freely. I want all genders, ethnic backgrounds and body types. Since some will be wearing team coveralls, I will need sizes. Deputy Sheriffs should be in their basic green uniforms."

"It sounds like you have done this before," a slightly grizzled state police captain says.

"Yes sir." Olivia is being intentionally curt. "What arrangements have been made concerning state and local dignitaries regarding protection?"

"We are only authorized to provide security for the governor, lieutenant governor and a few statutorily designated politicians," the state police captain replies. "Everyone else is on their own. Don't comp them. Let them be regular spectators."

"Billy," Sheriff McCarthy begins, "that's easier said than done. We have heard from the Orange County mayor's office and the City of Orlando mayor's office, plus a couple of commissioners, state reps and senators. I am waiting in fear for requests from members of the U.S. House and Senate."

"I can spare a few agents for them," Secret Service Agent Driver replies.

"Captain Wyler, can the state police lend me some undercover troopers?"

"I figured you'd ask Josh. You can have 40 members of our anti-terrorist task force. I would prefer that they be dressed in fatigues and be stationed at entrances and exits. It gives a presence that often can deter bad guys . . . especially amateurs."

"Aren't we going to extremes?' A young lawyer from the state Attorney General's office asks.

"May I answer?" I don't want to step on the toes of my superiors, but I recently wrote an article for a wire service regarding potential exposure to attacks at soft targets, especially car races where over 100,000 people attend.

"I know that several of you have met Detective Ballard, but his alter ego is that of one of the world's foremost automotive journalists, recognized in more countries than any of us . . . combined. This is his expertise. He knows the owners, the drivers, the crews, the media and he is a damn good cop. Go ahead Thomas."

"For some time law enforcement, together with intelligence agencies have viewed sporting events with large crowds as potentially soft targets. They are hard to control and contain. The Super Bowl in Miami was an example of everyone coming together to make the venue safe. And Captain, Detective Nederfield was loaned by our department to help coordinate security. The difference between this event and the Super Bowl is the international appeal of a Formula One race. The economic demographics of a football crowd and spectators at an F-1 are the difference between Bud Light and Moet. I am not being a snob, because I like Bud Light and I spend a lot more time at dirt tracks than I do attending mega-races, but it is fact. That makes this event not only a soft target, but very appealing to a deranged individual or a terrorist group. We haven't even started to talk about foreign dignitaries and corporate giants who will be in attendance."

"I am sorry Detective Ballard. I never realized the scope of this event. I am not much of a car guy." The young AG is trembling.

"You will be by the time this is over. This discussion would be moot if we had gotten some help from the legislature. The folks in Tallahassee need to pass a law which authorizes the Sheriff of a county to declare certain events, *no possession* events, applicable to every spectator, except law enforcement or those who are pre-approved by the event security chief, in this case Olivia. Unfortunately the legislature is not in session, so it won't happen, but law enforcement needs more tools."

"Josh, it won't fly." The state police captain doesn't sound too happy.

"Yup. But a patch work of designated venues isn't the answer. We need leadership at the state level. We don't want an international incident. Captain Wyler, we go back a long, long time, in fact, other than Thomas, I have known you longer than anyone else in law enforcement. If the shit hits the fan, so be it, but if it hits and we haven't done everything possible, we will all be painted the color brown. The track owners have agreed to ask the county commissioners for the designation for at least this event. Inasmuch as the Mayor of the county is a former cop, I think we will be okay."

"May I put a slight spin on this?" I ask. "I think we all agree that non-approved attendees should not carry personal firearms. Politicians, not otherwise afforded Secret Service or State protection present a relatively small problem. Treat them like regular attendees. Give them preferential seating if you feel it necessary, but not all together. While forbidding people who are not members of the law enforcement from possessing firearms should be easy, the state of Florida is gun crazy and we give out concealed weapons permits to anyone who can walk and chew gum at the same time, although there are some exceptions to even that qualification. It's easy to say that if you don't have a Florida gun permit, you can't carry a gun in Florida, but how do you say to some properly licensed individual that he or she cannot possess that which the law permits?"

"I am not totally following." The F.B. I. agent in attendance is simple to recognize: gray suit, white shirt; lightly starched, regimental tie, short haircut and reading glasses discreetly placed in his jacket pocket. "Why can't you simply ban guns?"

"Agent Whitmore, we do not have authority. It worked in Miami because the county commissioners designated the stadium as a no gun site. We don't have that luxury, although we may get a one-time nod. This is Florida and even after a school massacre, you can still buy a weapon at a gun show without a background check. I have seen too many homicides to be moved by arguments putting the rights of one person ahead of thousands. That is why the Sheriff wants legislation which fills in the loophole created by concealed weapon permit licenses. Let these *designated events* be safe and let security be in the hands of the professionals." Olivia is very passionate about her job—and other things as well.

"Although we have six weeks before the first activity associated with the race begins, we don't release the restriction until a week before the event. That will reduce any litigation potential. Everyone is used to the no cooler or no liquor rule, regardless whether we get the blessing from the commissioners, we will simply add another restriction. It will be a condition of admission to the events. From my point of view, I will simply send out a form to each person whom I accredit for media privileges to sign a waiver that they will not bring any firearm onto the property. If they don't agree, no press credentials. Easy." I think I am trying to convince myself as well as everyone else. Guns have been used to kill Presidents Lincoln, Garfield, McKinley, Kennedy and almost Ford and Reagan. Someone even took a pot shot at Teddy Roosevelt.

"Formula One is the most international motorsport event," I continue. "We have been flooded with VIP requests from foreign presidents, cabinet members, legislators and ministers, including some real heavy weights. First order of business is to limit the number of foreign dignitaries to real senior people in government. Then limit the number of tickets each gets, say four—spouse or friend and two body guards. We also have very limited secure seating areas. How do you accredit body guards from some of the countries that experience, shall we say, periodic government upheavals? We can't say the Prime Minister of England is okay but not the President of Haiti or a Saudi Prince."

"Since I have the task of putting all this together," Olivia begins, "I suggest that all body guards must be members of the military or national police force of their county, must be in uniform and may not carry a weapon."

Secret Service agent Driver asks, "Why should the foreign body guards be more conspicuous than our folks?"

"Good question with a simple answer. I want to be able to easily pick out theirs from ours. I can only vet these folks superficially," Olivia points out. "Basically, I don't trust most foreign protection personnel. I think that ruffling a few feathers is better than an international incident. Can we vouch-safe the security personnel from certain Baltic countries? How many times have we heard about a political leader traveling abroad and his own people do him harm as part of a coup. I want to be able to demand that all foreign security forces wear either military or law enforcement uniforms. We can't make exceptions. It may cause some flack, but I'm a big girl and can take the hit. Noncompliance means non-attendance." Chief Detective Nederfield returns to her seat. The collective law enforcement group assembled is speechless.

"You can now undoubtedly see why Olivia Nederfield is my chief detective. She speaks her mind which is refreshing, not always political correct, but almost always spot on," Sheriff McCarthy inserts.

"What do you mean almost always spot on?" Olivia's quip breaks the tension.

CHAPTER TWO

"I don't know about you, but I am totally wasted. Talking about guns and terrorism is depressing . . . and it diminishes a lot of the excitement about the race." I hope I am not sounding like a wimp.

"Thomas, you are car guy first and a cop guy second, but in the crazy world in which we live we need to over prepare. Look at it this way, by doing what we are doing; the automotive world will have a fantastic and safe experience."

"Now I know why I love you."

"I thought you loved me because I am incredibly beautiful and sexy."

"That, too. I think we should go out for dinner at *Joe and Joanne's,* have a huge Caesar salad with garlic bread and a couple of glasses of vin ordinaire and retire early."

"Retire early? What does that imply?" Olivia is trying to stifle a laugh.

"Whatever you wish," I adroitly reply.

"Let me give it some thought while I am taking a shower. And a cold beer would be appreciated upon completion of my cleansing ritual." Olivia wiggles in just the right places and heads off to our rather oversized bathroom.

"Shall I join you?" I quip.

"I think you should wash up in the outside shower," she replies.

"We don't have an outside shower."

"Then I suggest you should spend the time during which I have exclusive use of the bathroom planning how to install an outside shower." Olivia waves and closes the door.

Actually I think an outside shower is a cool idea. I wonder what the neighbors would think. In our neighborhood, probably nothing. I open the refrigerator and remove a frosty PBR. I open the patio door, grab several newspapers and decide to put my down time to good use. I need to send some story lines to the news wires about the logistic planning for the race, concentrating on the wonderful transportation options available and ignoring the potential threat to life and limb.

I bash out a few pithy sentences, finish my beer, glance through the various sports sections, type in notes from today's meeting, avoid my email and get up to roust Olivia before she uses up all the hot water.

My knock on the door is immediately answered by a vision that takes my breath away. Olivia has wrapped a towel around her hair, but is otherwise in the altogether. "You may look, but don't touch. You are dirty and smelly from today. As I recall you said something about retiring early. Patience is a virtue." Olivia grabs an over sized robe and walks right past me into the bedroom. I sublimate the urge to follow her. She has already laid down the ground rules. I can live with that—more or less.

I must admit that a hot shower is a real pick me up. I wonder what reaction I would get if I walked into the bedroom with a towel wrapped around my head and nothing else.

Probably mass hysteria and then I would feel bad and my confidence would be shot—figuratively speaking. I grab the remaining terrycloth bathrobe and discreetly knock on the bedroom door. Detective Nederfield slowly opens the door.

"Tah Dah," she says. Olivia is wearing a pair of jeans that must have been spray painted onto her gorgeous body and a work shirt which she wears untucked.

"Looking good my lady. Looking good."

"Shake a tail feather Mr. Ballard. I am famished and wish to retire early."

Should I suggest skipping dinner and getting right to the retiring early part? Patience is a virtue.

"Ready," I announce. My ensemble is very pedestrian; chinos, freshly pressed, and a light green linen shirt, also untucked.

Olivia offers me her arm, which I take with pleasure. After turning on the home security system, checking it with my cell phone and locking the door. We are ready for a three block stroll to the restaurant. One of the things I like about urban living is the proximity of so much variety.

Joe and Joanne's specializes in good food, good wine, nice ambiance and fair prices. There are a number of tables on the sidewalk patio, but we opt to eat inside. I open the door and Joe immediately says from across the room, "Olivia and Thomas, my two favorite cops. Welcome!"

Usually that kind of greeting gets no reaction in our neighborhood because our occupation is well know and sometimes Olivia has parked a marked Sheriff's Ford Explorer in front on the house. The folks living around us kind of like the protective feeling. However, within an instant after Joe greeted us, I noticed three guys sitting in the back begin to squirm. Rather than draw attention to them I walk over to Joanne who has just come from the kitchen and give her a big hug.

"Where would you two love birds like to sit?" Joanne asks.

"It's a beautiful evening, how about a table outside on the patio?" I give Olivia's ankle a quick kick. She smiles at me, but her eyes quickly case the restaurant.

We are escorted to an outside table. "Some wine?" Joanne asks.

"Yes, please," Olivia replies. She begins to text. Normally we do not even have our cell phones on the table during a meal, but this is business.

"Josh?" I ask, referring to the Sheriff.

"I am glad you are so observant. Two of those thugs have outstanding warrants for a drug and weapons charges. Dangerous. I don't recognize the third. Backup will be here shortly."

I start to write on the back of my business card—*Joe and Joanne—guys in back of restaurant are wanted—be careful. Unlock back door.*

Our drinks arrive and I place my note on top of a $20 bill which I put on Joanne's tray.

"Aren't you having dinner?" she asks.

"Maybe later. Please read the note on the back of the card." She does. To her credit, not a muscle twitches.

"I'll bring you menus in case you change your mind." She turns and leaves.

Two rather noisy younger couples arrive and enter the restaurant.

"Two are from vice and two from narcotics. Real good deputies." Olivia raises her glass. "Cheers!" We clink and sip.

"I think I am going to go to the men's room and check out the back door," I announce.

"Actually, I'm going to the ladies' room. I assume you are not in possession of a firearm. I am. End of conversation." Olivia rises. So do I, but only as a gentleman. I sit after she enters the restaurant.

Out of the corner of my eye, I see several familiar faces from the Sheriff's office, including the big guy himself with a petite red head on his arm. Josh is happily married and I happen to know that his *date* is an instructor in martial arts. I'm bored, but not stupid. I am not an OK Corral type of deputy. I'm more of a nerd. After about five minutes, I switch from bored to worried. Maybe I should go in. Luckily for me, Olivia opens the door and returns to her seat.

"I saved your wine." I want to be light, but not trite.

"You didn't miss a thing. The third person at the table was an undercover Fed. Good thing Billy Spencer from our office recognized him. Nancy, you know the woman with Josh, made a scene and started pushing the Boss away. One of the guys stood up to help a damsel in distress and she decked him. Out cold. In the blink of an eye at least five weapons were pointing at the second thug and at the undercover guy, so that his cover wasn't blown. Everyone was packed into a van waiting out back and whoosh, off to the county jail.

"May we join you?" When the voice comes from a bear of a man, you always say *yes*. When it comes from the Sheriff, you say *yes, sir*. When it comes from your oldest and best friend, you say *pull up a chair*.

"The power of observation of members of the fourth estate should never be underestimated. Olivia and Thomas, I want you to meet Lieutenant Nancy Johns, who heads up our martial arts training program."

"I saw you in action. Maybe I should come in for a refresher course," Olivia replies.

"Then you will have to teach me all about weapons. Sheriff McCarthy said you were one of the best in the state."

"Deal!" The two women shake hands.

Joanne comes rushing out and says, some guests think that was part of a new nightly entertainment act we have. It was so perfect. "Thank you all. What can I get you to drink?"

"We are all off duty," announces Sheriff McCarthy. "I'll have a Maker's Mark with a single ice cube and a Dr. Pepper. Lieutenant?"

"May I have a double espresso? It calms my nerves."

"You must have nerves of steel," I observe.

"Olivia, Thomas, another wine?" Joanne asks.

We nod. "And some of your delicious fresh bread with olive oil and basil," Detective Nederfield almost shot a bad guy, but her appetite is undeterred.

"I guess the department owes you guys a dinner inasmuch as yours was interrupted. Under cover surveillance we'll call it. I am sure Helen will approve the requisition." Josh starts to laugh. Helen is his executive assistant, tough as nails with over thirty years of police work under her belt. Everyone knows she runs the place.

"You are too kind," Olivia sarcastically replies.

"Yes, I know. Time to head home. Dinner is awaiting. Lieutenant, shall I take you back to headquarters?"

"No thank you Sheriff. I'll just sit for a few minutes if it is okay with you Olivia . . . Thomas. I need the adrenaline level to lower a bit," she replies.

"We'd love to have you join us. We are probably going to split an order of eggplant parmesan and maybe have another glass of wine. The food here is excellent, but the portions are huge, so if you are not too hungry, I'll ask Joanne to make it a double order and there will even be enough to take some home." Olivia is trying to make Nancy Johns comfortable.

After almost an hour of chit chat about everything except law enforcement, and the consumption of a giant plate of food, I think Olivia has a new best friend. Well not quite a best friend, if you know what I mean.

CHAPTER THREE

"So much for the peaceful, romantic dinner," I quip as we walk back to the house.

"I think we are going to have to go to a sun drenched island to escape . . . for at least two weeks," Olivia replies.

"Shall we pack tonight or tomorrow morning?"

"I thought you had something in mind for tonight." The gorgeous detective leans over to give me a kiss.

"I thought that after all the excitement that you may want to take a rain check." I guess that the evening's events are beginning to sink in.

"Thomas, that's why I love you. You are actually quite thoughtful and sensitive . . . for a man. And lest we forget, there's always tomorrow."

"That would make a good title for a book," I respond. Olivia slips her arm around my waist and we walk in silence.

"Let's get ready for bed and snuggle," Olivia suggests after we enter our humble residence.

"Hanky panky will have to wait. I think we are both on the same wave length."

The morning comes way too early. Wait! It's only 6 o'clock. Damn phone. I roll over to retrieve my cell from the night stand. "It's the ogre," I announce, referring to our boss.

"What could he possibly want this early? Does he ever sleep?" Olivia is as annoyed as I am.

"First you ruin our dinner and now our sleep," I shout into the phone.

"Good morning Thomas. Put me on speaker." Josh sounds disgustingly cheerful.

I push the speaker button. "Yeh?"

"Hi guys. Got some news. The assistant Secretary of State is flying in to meet with us. Apparently the guest list of celebrities for the F-1 race is expanding and it appears that we may be hosting several world leaders, including both the President and Vice President," Sheriff McCarthy relates.

Although I am still groggy, I say, "I thought that Air Force One and Air Force Two are never together at an event like this." Olivia nods in assent.

"Me, too. I am not sure what's up except that we are meeting with these folks at 11 in my office."

"Who exactly are these folks?" I ask.

"Not sure, but I sense that we will be meeting with major players at State, Homeland Security, FBI and Secret Service. I am rounding up Sheriff Wetherford from Volusia County and will try to get someone from Florida Department of Law Enforcement."

"This is getting a bit above my pay grade," I whisper to Olivia.

"I heard that Thomas. Everything is above your pay grade. I don't pay you anything," Josh growls.

"Touché!"

"We will hold up our end. I think adding Mike Wetherford to the mix is a good idea," Detective Nederfield adds.

"See you at 11." Sheriff McCarthy ends the call.

By the way, Mike is the sheriff of the county adjoining Orange County and is a full blooded Seminole native Floridian, raised in the Everglades and probably the most intuitive person I have ever met. And also the toughest.

"Shall we try and get more sleep or face the day?" I ask.

"Let's put in a couple of miles, have some grapefruit and toast on the deck and then take a shower," Olivia answers.

"Together?" My perfectly reasonable question is countered by a punch to the arm. Not too hard, but the message was clear—patience.

It is always best to jog in the morning in Florida. Within hours of sun rise the temperature can often reach 90 or more. In the late afternoon, you are often greeted with thunder and lightning and rain. Also, aerobic exercise is supposed to be good for you, but then again, so is a glass or two of red wine. Go figure.

As we establish the pace, our movement becomes automatic. It occurs to me that Josh's early morning call has all the earmarks of a disaster. Where can you safely seat all those world leaders and presumably their entourage at a race track? It's a nightmare. Although the developers of the facility installed beautiful luxury boxes from which to view events, other than the so-called *owner's box*, the rest of the seats have been sold to captains of industry, entertainment or sports. I sure don't want to tell them that they can't have their bought and paid for preferred seating at the venues biggest race because the POTUS wants to show off to other big wigs. That's a no win situation for sure. I know that there are only a handful of seats not already committed which we were planning to use for the team owners and sponsors. What a revolting circumstance this is turning out to be.

"If we are hosting the G-7 summit at the race track, we are in way over our heads," I comment.

"That my love is a gross understatement. If we thought transportation issues were dicey, what do we do with limousines, helicopters and armored personnel carriers?" Olivia asks.

"Do they really have armored personnel carriers?"

"I have never done security at that level, but it wouldn't surprise me a bit," she replies.

"We have been talking about soft targets for terrorist activity, but we haven't even considered problems still existent regarding social distancing and masks. The vaccine seems to be effective, but are we going to make everyone show their medical certificate before entering the facility?"

"You raise an issue that has been bothering me. Everyone seems to have a short memory, especially in light of the international makeup of the event. I am going to call Josh and ask him to consider getting Public Health involved, especially if all of the world's leaders converge on Central Florida . . . in six weeks. I think I am going back to bed for a couple of months."

"Thomas, you are a baby. Law enforcement members are skilled and prepared to handle anything including terrorism, the plague, 100,000 spectators and their personal transportation modules. Not!"

"I like the personal transportation module touch. Olivia, this has all the potential of being catastrophic."

"It is our job to prevent it from becoming so. I would love to have a couple more months of planning, about a zillion dollars for infrastructure and an army of security, logistic and medical personnel. Then I might feel less petrified."

I have never seen Olivia express fear of any sort.

"Josh's meeting sounds like a coat and tie affair," I grumble.

"Sweetheart, this is Central Florida. No one wears a tie. Chinos, a nice dress shirt open at the collar and your new linen sports coat and you will be the most fashionable guy there. Shall I wear my badge on a silver chain or a faux gold chain?"

"Clip it to your belt. You don't want to draw attention to the fact that it is from a Cracker Jack box."

"You can be so hurtful. Just because yours is gold and mine is kind of dull silver, you don't need to rub it in." We are both trying not to laugh.

"I have the answer," Olivia shouts. "Wear your Associated Press badge around your neck. That is sure to get attention."

"Hah, hah! Maybe I'll wear those Seminole war beads Mike gave me. That will do the trick."

"Unless Sheriff Wetherford wears his deerskin fringed jacket."

"As long as he doesn't bring his tomahawk," I reply.

Although we are making fun of our dear friend, he carries a 12 inch Bowie knife on his service belt along with the issue Glock and Mike frequently is shod in homemade moccasins. I guess when you are 6'5" you don't need boots to make you taller. We are both trying to avoid thinking about the potential disaster that awaits us.

"It's going to be a nice day so let's take my car," Olivia offers. "Maybe we can drive over to the beach for dinner."

"You are assuming that we will ever get out of the meeting."

"Good point, Thomas. We better come up with some really good answers."

"I don't even want to know the questions."

"I have to admit, this has gotten above my pay grade as well. What I fear most is that the suits will come up with some crazy plan and leave it to us to implement their vision without the resources we need. We have completely ignored health issues."

"Darling, lest I be a spoil sport, we will have spectators, as well as media from Italy, Spain and Brazil as well as the Far East and we haven't spent two minutes talking about anything but guns. I think we can do a good job at providing security for things we can see, but I am not sure about things we cannot see."

"Thomas, you are scaring me . . . and I am not easily frightened as you well know. I'm going to call Sheriff McCarthy. Not only do we need a public health expert, but we need the mayors of both Orlando and Orange County at the meeting."

"Agreed." The division of political power in Central Florida is confusing. Suffice it to say that the two mayors have concurrent jurisdiction and overlapping responsibilities. We are lucky, however. The mayor of Orange County was the sheriff immediately before Josh got the job. He is so calm that those who oppose him are lulled into a sense of advantage. Big mistake. The mayor of Orlando is a fifth generation native of the city. Her father was the pastor of one of Central Florida's largest congregations and was the leading force backing the city's inclusion policy. Mayor Dixon went to divinity school and was going to follow in her father's footsteps, but got another calling: politics. She has served four terms and is so well regarded that she now runs unopposed.

"I wish we had a little more time to prepare for this meeting. I don't think I should wear my press credentials. I might get thrown out on my ear." Is the world really ready for international gatherings? It hasn't been that long since we were all under *stay at home orders*. I guess I shouldn't be surprised that the issue hasn't been raised before. Everyone wants to get back to normal. If we waive the flag, are we opening Pandora's Box? As a member of the fourth estate, I feel conflicted. I search for the facts and report them, but my venue is car racing and this is the largest event ever to visit Central Florida. Are my concerns real or hyped?

"Thomas, are you alright?" Olivia wakes me from contemplating the world at large.

"I'm scared, too. Our job is to serve and protect. What if we conclude that we cannot protect, do we then not serve?"

"If it weren't 8 o'clock in the morning, I'd tell you to go to bed and sleep on it, but . . ."

"Great idea! Care to join me?" My remark results in a punch to the arm and a really nice kiss to the lips.

CHAPTER FOUR

The morning sun is bright and the sky is blue, so we lower the top on Olivia's perfectly restored VW bug. It's only about five miles as the crow flies to the Orange County Sheriff's headquarters and adjacent jail. However, crows don't do well in Central Florida and neither does the traffic. Our journey takes over one-half hour. Then there is parking. Fortunately, Chief Detective Nederfield has her own space only a short walk from the elevator. One would think that parking in the garage at the Sheriff's Department would be the safest spot in town. Actually it probably is, but that being said, we raise the top, roll up the windows, lock the doors and set the car alarm.

"I want to run a comb threw my hair and check my office. Shall I check to see if you have any messages?"

"I should say *no thank you*, but there may be some media members who don't know how to email but want to curse me, urge me to approve their credentials or otherwise want to ruin my day." I actually have an office at headquarters, if you call a broom closet with a desk, a chair, and a telephone a real office.

The large conference room adjacent to Josh's office is on the top (fifth) floor, while our offices are on the second.

Olivia has a decent view of Orlando's urban sprawl while I have a view of nothing. Truth be known, I don't have a window at all. It all works out because if I had a nice office, I might feel guilty if I didn't visit every once in a while. Olivia leaves me alone to travel the remaining three stories. At least the architects of the new headquarters had the decency not to include piped in music.

Rather than make a grand entrance, I sneak into Josh's office and blow Helen a kiss. She responds with a wave and a finger pointing to Sheriff McCarthy's inner sanctum. I knock.

"Come on in Thomas. I have a cup of tea for you." He sounds way too cheery. Maybe I should be worried.

"Good morning . . . again . . . great exalted one. What is the word on the street?" I try to sound cheery as well.

"Where's Olivia?"

"Trying to get a comb through her hair."

"You must have driven her car," Josh replies.

"I've known you for over forty years and what I have learned is that you only make small talk if you are angry or scared . . . usually the former."

"How about both?"

"That bad?" I ask.

"Yup."

We are interrupted by a knock on the boss's door.

"Enter at your own peril," I shout.

Sometimes you see something that takes your breath away. Sheriff Mike and Detective Olivia enter the room together. They are incredibly-breath taking. Olivia's height is augmented by her sensible walking shoes, closely tailored suit and perfect posture. Mike doesn't need his height augmented. Not only is he wearing his signature fringed jacket but has added knee high beaded deerskin boots. At least there are no scalps hanging from his belt, but neither is the Bowie knife.

"Welcome. As you can imagine the Feds have insisted that no one is armed." The contrast between Josh in his forest green starched and pressed uniform with four stars on the collar and Mike, who if he wasn't the real McCoy, looks like someone from central casting, is almost comical. "Mike you are not carrying, are you?" Josh sounds nervous.

"Don't need white man's thunder stick to be secure." Everyone breaks out laughing so hard that Helen rushes in.

"Don't you four have something better to do than to scare an old lady?"

Mike looks down at his feet. "Sorry Miss Helen." Now all five of us have tears running down our cheeks.

While we are carrying on like a bunch of little kids, Orange County Mayor Clement and Orlando Mayor the Reverend Dixon walk into the boss's office.

"Anyone wish to share the joke?" Former Sheriff Clement asks.

"It might lose something in translation," I quip.

"Is that to or from English Deputy Ballard?" I didn't think that the Mayor knew my name. Fortunately our exchange gave the others a chance to collect their breath and gather their wits.

"Sorry, but things are getting a little tense and we were blowing off steam before we find out what kind of deep dung we are in." I think Sheriff Wetherford has summed up our behavior accurately.

"Based on your footwear, I gather that it's pretty deep." Mayor Clement smiles from ear to ear.

"Helen, if you could have someone rustle up some coffee, I will lead us in a prayer for deliverance from the D.C. suits." Mayor Dixon also has a great sense of humor.

"Boss," Olivia begins, "were you able to get someone from public health?"

"She is on her way. Dr. Lucille Hastings is as good as it gets."

"If this thing gets out of control, I am more than willing to declare another *stay at home* order. Regardless of whether we have a pandemic, a threat of a pandemic, and a couple of sniffles or whatever." You can tell that Mayor Clement is not kidding. An event of this magnitude takes years to plan and if a monkey wrench gets thrown into that plan, figuratively speaking, I'll pull the plug and take the heat."

"Virgil, I've known you a long time. I was proud to succeed you in this office, but if it hits the fan I'll take the heat with you."

Wow!

"Gentlemen, you will not be standing alone. The entire city of Orlando will back you," Mayor Dixon adds.

"I will make sure Volusia County grants you asylum." Mike Wetherford inserts with a smile.

"I'll make sure the press is fully informed. Maybe I'll get on the Today Show." Olivia punches me in the arm and everyone laughs.

"I guess I'm stuck with getting coffee." Helen salutes and leaves.

I feel good about our team. We will do our jobs only if we can do them well. My thoughts are interrupted by Sheriff's McCarthy's private phone ringing.

He picks it up and listens. "Please show them to the large conference room. There is coffee, soft drinks, and water as well as some muffins and bagels. I'll be there in ten minutes . . . after our prayer meeting." Everyone is trying not to break out in gales of laughter.

"Who was that on the phone?" I ask. "I hope it wasn't that nice intern from UCF. He will be blown away."

"When the going gets tough . . ."

"Our beloved leader and friend grabs a Dr. Pepper." Obviously Mike and Josh are pretty close.

After making our uninvited guests wait a socially correct ten minutes, we enter the conference room. If I didn't have great self control, I would most likely start laughing. Six white males, all dressed in basic gray or dark blue suits, each wearing Windsor knotted ties, greet us. Other than Donald Driver, who is standing a few feet away from the rest, I do not recognize anyone.

"Welcome to Orlando," Sheriff McCarthy bellows. "I'd like to welcome you to our team." His introduction is interrupted by Helen knocking at the door.

"Sheriff, Dr. Hastings has arrived." She steps aside. Dr. Hastings exudes a no nonsense demeanor.

"Let me introduce you to Dr. Lucille Hastings, who is a professor of infectious disease at the University of Florida Medical School and a special consultant to our esteemed mayors, the Reverend Doris Dixon and former Orange County Sheriff Virgil Clement. As you have already gathered, I am Sheriff Josh McCarthy and to my right is Volusia County Sheriff Mike Wetherford. To his right is my Chief Detective Olivia Nederfield and last but not least is Special Deputy Thomas Ballard.

"Sheriff, I thought it was understood that this meeting is private. The press is not welcome."

"I'm sorry, but who the hell are you?" Josh's voice is really a growl.

"My name is Tyler Harrison III. I am the deputy assistant Secretary of State."

"Mr. Harrison, you are my guest so I won't tell you that you are a haughty pup. I am willing to hear what you and your colleagues have to say, but I do not take orders from anyone in my office. Is that understood?"

Harrison nods and before he opens his mouth again, another suit says, "I am sorry Sheriff, we are all under a lot of pressure from the White House. Oh, my name is William Douglas and I am with the Department of Homeland Security. My associates are from right to left, Chuck Stoddard from the office of the Attorney General; Kent Forbes from the FBI, Nicholas Tsarkis, the President's assistant Chief of Staff and Dan Driver from the Secret Service, who I understand you have met. I am sorry we have already started off on the wrong foot."

"Mr. Harrison seems to know me as a journalist, but I am also a Deputy Sheriff serving the people of Orange County where I was born. My father was a plumber here and so was my grandfather. Mayor Dixon's roots in Central Florida go back five generations and those of Sheriff Wetherford go back to the beginning of time. Sheriff McCarthy's father was the Chief of Police in Orlando. Before becoming the Sheriff, Mayor Clemont served as a Navy SEAL leader for twenty years. Chief Detective Nederfield is the daughter of an immigrant who fled Nazi Germany and who graduated first in her class from the police academy. I hope you come to realize that my persona as an automotive journalist makes me uniquely positioned. Simply said, I know all the players and more importantly they know me and trust me."

Ashen is the best way to describe Deputy Assistant Secretary of State Harrison.

"Sheriff McCarthy, may I?" Secret Service regional director Driver asks.

"Of course, Dan."

"My colleagues from the Nation's Capital truly believe that everything ends at the beltway, including competence. Let me assure them that the group before you represents well over a century of experience and expertise. The folks have been involved in and have successfully resolved situations with major international law enforcement implications. Their access to resources, both traditional and somewhat unorthodox, is only whispered about. This is their bailiwick and we would be best to acknowledge that now."

Now all the suits have an ashen pallor.

"I think that we had better get a move on it while the sun is still high in the sky." Mike loves his homilies.

"I am the chief of security for the race, so tell us what you have in mind." Olivia sounds impatient and a little pissed off.

"I think that I can be straightforward with you. POTUS is hosting a mini G-7 conference in Palm Beach and wants to invite the participants to the race." I must admit that Mr. Tsarkis has summed up the issue succinctly.

"No can do," I blurt out. "I may be a humble member of the fourth estate, but what you are asking cannot be done for a myriad of reasons. Let me start with the simple ones: where do you think these world leaders can be seated?"

"Don't you have skyboxes which would be easily secured?" Forbes from the FBI asks.

"The track does have twelve special seating areas along the main straightaway. Each box has fifty seats," I start.

"There you go!" Agent Forbes interrupts.

"And each seat has an owner," I finish.

"Can't you get them to move?" Apparently Deputy Assistant Secretary Harrison has recovered his voice.

"First of all, it is not our call. Nor is it the call of the organizers of the race, which has been planned for over two years. It is the call of each individual owner or corporate owner, which includes Fortune 500 companies, members of the Forbes most wealthy list and ordinary people who have waited a lifetime for this event. There are about twenty seats that have been set aside for team owners and sponsors. There isn't a room or a seat at the inn."

"That's not our problem, it's yours." Harrison is beginning to froth at the mouth.

"Sit down and shut up!" Mayor Dixon sounds like a stevedore. "I will ask Sheriff McCarthy to have you removed. I thought Thomas made it clear, we will look for solutions, but we will not tolerate demands."

"Let me make one thing perfectly clear." When a former SEAL speaks, everyone listens. "Mayor Dixon and I are empowered to cancel the event especially if we think there might be a threat to public health and Dr. Hastings has assured me that hosting tens of thousands people from all over the world is already pushing the social distancing envelope. So don't even think about threatening us with anything."

"This is not going well," Mr. Tsarkis discerns.

"Let's start from the beginning," I suggest. "The President wants to host his guests at the largest automotive event in the world . . . on six weeks notice. Right?"

"Well put, Thomas." Sheriff Wetherford has been uncharacteristically quiet. Actually so has Sheriff McCarthy.

Olivia rises from her seat, leans forward and places her hands flat on the conference table. "I am the only one here, I surmise, who has ever organized security for a public event of the size we expect and within the confines of a closed environment. Forget about seating, forget about the virus, we are having a tough enough time trying to make those who we already know are coming safe and secure. Is everyone going to have to pass through a security portal? Yes! Is everyone going to have to get their temperature checked? Yes! Are we going to have to do this for all four days of the event? Yes again! This is already a nightmare. Imagine inserting the President of the United States and the rest of the leaders of the world in this environment. Thomas, I certainly hope our friends from Washington have read your articles or attended your lectures about soft targets at sporting events, especially race tracks. If they had, then they would know what I am saying. Sure, Presidents have attended major sporting events, but that was before COVID 19; before the riots; and before sophisticated and hard to detect tools of destruction were widely available."

"I have an idea! It is actually quite brilliant if I do say so myself."

"The humble journalist speaks," Josh chortles.

"I pose the following question: what are the real, deep and underlying motives of the President for attending the event? We know he's no fan of cars in general and racing in particular. What we are about to say, from both sides, stays in this room, so I want candid responses. Let me suggest that POTUS simply wants to impress the attendees. Maybe that is a bit harsh, let's assume he wants to show off our great country as host of the world's most important automotive event. He is in South Florida and the race is in Central Florida. Why not bring the race to him?"

"What are you talking about Thomas?" Olivia's voice is about an octave higher than normal.

"What if I convince the event organizers to have an exhibition and a meet and greet session at the race track near Palm Beach? A closed affair with no spectators and only limited press."

"Present company excluded," my Seminole friend inserts, bringing a chuckled to the assembled.

"Wait a minute!" Assistant Chief of Staff Tsarkis announces. "Mr. Ballard is right. This is brilliant, if indeed it is possible."

"I think we need a plan and certain agreements in place before making phone calls. First I need a commitment everyone will work under the aegis of Sheriffs McCarthy and Wetherford . . ."

"And Sheriff Rosewood," Mike adds.

"Who is Sheriff Rosewood?" Agent Forbes asks.

"He is the Sheriff of Palm Beach County . . . and my cousin," Mike replies.

"Second," I continue, "I am going to need a lot of resources, both in terms of personnel and money. We will need to provide the driver's and owners something more than a photo op to get them to go to Palm Beach and then return to Orlando. And I am going to need both FBI and Secret Service agents all over the place. I assume we can get help from Palm Beach County."

"Thomas, you have raised an interesting point and one which might be just the hook that we need. Other than reimbursing the teams for additional out of pocket expenses, which would be far less than the cost of bringing the G-7 participants from Palm Beach to Orlando and back, I want there to be a cause to which the teams can make a donation of their incentive money. Is there a foundation for retired or disabled drivers?"

"Madam Mayor, I yield the brilliant idea trophy to you," I say.

"Thank you scribe of the roar of thunder and the dripping of oil in my garage."

Now everyone, with the possible exception of Tyler Harrison III, is smiling.

"I agree that the Bureau will work with you, actually under your direction, provided you don't tell anyone." Agent Forbes is with the program.

"Needless to say, the Secret Service is on board."

"Thanks, Dan," the Sheriffs say together.

Olivia raises her hand. "I need a lot more facial recognition software along with technicians. I want both hand held and fixed security screener units and trained personnel. Without sounding over reacting, I would like some dogs, especially in Palm Beach. I still have an event to run here over four days and I assume I will have to be in Palm Beach as well."

"Homeland Security at your service. I will send down one of our best party planners."

"Can I request digital units to monitor temperature?" Dr. Hastings asks.

"Actually I was hoping you would put together complete protocols for both events, applicable for both spectators and participants," Josh replies.

"Of course. Next Monday?"

"Thomas, can you distribute the protocols to all the teams? Let them know there will be no exceptions."

"I will send them out to the media as well and ask that my colleagues include the protocols in articles they write about the event."

"This brings me to a very sensitive subject," Chief Detective Nederfield speaks in a measured voice. "Mayor Clement, I have a request. It will not be well received by many, but it will go a long way to making sure everyone is safe."

"Let me respond before you even ask. Doris and I have been talking about issuing executive orders which we will have ratified by the County Commissioners and City Council, declaring the event venue a no carry zone. We are going to basically copy the Miami-Dade regulation since it survived several legal challenges and I am not in the mood to reinvent the wheel. Did that answer your unasked question, Chief Detective?"

Olivia demurely smiles. "You have made my life a lot easier. Thomas, please have the media circulate the executive orders as well. And there will be no exceptions except for law enforcement. Private security will have to be unarmed. I could hug you both."

"I'd accept," Mayor Clement begins, "but Deputy Ballard might have me arrested for indecent behavior." Everyone, even Deputy Assistant Secretary of State Harrison, begins to laugh.

"Well done Virgil . . . Doris," Sheriff McCarthy looks relieved. "You have added several years to my quickly fleeting life."

We are interrupted by a knock. Without waiting for a reply, Helen enters. "Since an army cannot run on empty stomachs, I have reserved the back room at Houlihan's for lunch in about thirty minutes. Sheriff Mike will Sheriff Rosewood be joining us?" The word *us* was not lost on me.

Helen attends all high level meetings, especially if it involves Irish stew.

"Does the FBI have a plane at Palm Beach airport that could bring my cousin here? I want you to meet him since we now have dual venues."

"Let me check," Agent Forbes replies. He stands and moves to the far end of the room, presumably because it is quiet, but with the Feds, one never knows. To his credit the call take less than three minutes. "Hanger number 104 on the executive side. I will confirm once you get the okay from Sheriff Rosewood."

Mike is already dialing. "Eyaha? It's Tall Tree. Can you be available for a meeting in Orlando in about forty minutes? A plane is waiting at the airport. Hanger 104 on the executive side." Sheriff Wetherford listens. "Call me en route. Josh will have a car." Another pause. "No, Detective Nederfield will not pick you up. *Aeepa-ischay.*"

"Elias is still incorrigible ever since I beat him at the Sheriffs' Association marksmanship event two years ago." Olivia says. Her comment is met with surprise by several of the suits, but not by Dan Driver. His unit regularly participates in active shooting programs developed and led by Olivia.

"I think we need to use the next half hour to go over several key details, like getting a list of everyone who is planning to attend the event at Palm Beach, both guests and participants. The Secret Service will be responsible for vetting the guests and the FBI will get the participants, most of whom will be the same on the Citrus Grove list. Mr. Tsarkis, there will have to be some limit to the number of people in each G-7 member's entourage. I suggest no more than ten. Is that going to work?"

"Deputy Ballard . . ."

"Thomas."

"Thomas, it will have to work. The President is head-strong, but pragmatic. It is either your way or, based on Mayor Clement, the highway. And actually, the new plan fulfills both ego and positive image. I will pull the list together and get it to the Secret Service with copies to everyone here. I think the less that is said about the Palm Beach event, the better until we are a little closer to finalizing plans."

Everyone is getting into the game. Now the only thing I have to do is convince Charles Shaw, owner of the Gold Coast Raceway, to rent us the track for a couple of days, convince owners, crews and drivers that a relaxing day in Palm Beach is a good idea, get Mike's cousin on board, choreograph everything here and there, make sure that Olivia has all the help she needs, make sure Dr. Hastings is getting sufficient resources, make sure the medical protocols and no firearms orders are disseminated, finishing vetting the media applications, and pray to the rain gods to stay away.

What have I forgotten? I am sure there's something or many somethings. I actually feel like we have accomplished a lot. What time is it? I'm getting hungry.

CHAPTER FIVE

At the appointed hour we all take leave of *the house that Josh built*, and walk about a block to Houlihan's, the best Irish cop bar south of Dublin, and that includes Boston and New York. Run by retired State Police Captain, Sean Dooley and his dear, sweet mother, who everyone calls *Ma*, Houlihan's is dark, warm and friendly. Darts are played 24/7 and every Wednesday is open mic. Some of the best music ever. Ma is in charge of the kitchen and there are no menus. You are served what she thinks you should eat. I remember when Josh and I were about ten, his dad, who was not yet chief of police, brought us to Houlihan's for our first lager and lime. How cool was that?

I think the suits are a bit overwhelmed, but quite sub-dued as we are led to the back room. "Pints all around?" Sean asks.

I have the feeling the deputy assistant secretary of state was about to decline, until he was kicked in the ankle by Charles Stoddard, from whom we have heard nothing. "I'd like a black and tan and so would my colleague." I like the guy already. The ladies order Harp and the rest of us have Guinness. Sean leaves and Ma enters. She immediately gives us all a hug and says to the Beltway crowd, "Welcome to Houlihan's. Today we are serving Corned Beef and cabbage, Irish stew and Shepherd's pie. I'll bring out some fresh rolls while you stew over the choices." She giggles at her joke. As she is about to leave she screams, "Saints be with us!" Sheriff Elias Rosewood is standing at the door. He is the spitting image of Mike except he is wearing an embroidered denim shirt and jeans.

"Ma, it's been far too long. He leans down and sweeps her up into his arms and kisses each of her rosy cheeks.

"Put me down you savage . . . and let me have a look at you." Ma is the sweetest person I have ever met. "You can take the boy out of the 'Glades, but you can't take the 'Glades out of the boy." She repeats the menu to Sheriff Rosewood and bustles out.

"Gentlemen, this is Elias Rosewood, Sheriff of Palm Beach County," I announce. "He is pretty much up to speed."

"How?" Tyler Harrison III spits out.

"That's my line," Elias replies. "But while I was flying up here, Helen gave me most of the highlights. I also gave Brother Shaw a call and told him the County wants to rent the entire track for the Monday prior to the race. He didn't put it together. He thinks we are running a driver's school for local law enforcement. I am sending one of my deputies over to the track to get the contract and give him a deposit. We are going to be reimbursed, aren't we?"

Nicholas Tsarkis nods and smiles. "Your team is exceedingly efficient. Quite frankly, I am used to working with people with little or no initiative. While you may be local, you are very professional. I feel a lot better and whole heartedly will follow your lead."

Before any of us could respond, Sean enters with a tray filled with pints of ambrosia. We placed our food orders and raised our collective glasses.

"To a far better solution to the problem than I ever imagined." The President's deputy chief of staff looks relieved as well as pleased. "Thank you. Cheers."

How Ma can create so many meals, so quickly in her tiny kitchen may be attributed to the fact that she was raised with eight siblings. There are few words in the English language that describe the aroma surrounding out lunch.

After everyone is done eating or rather shoveling food into their mouths, Sheriff Wetherford rises and says, "To Ma, *is-tee-hull-wash*."

"My Seminole, actually Muscogee, is a bit rusty. Would either of you indigenous persons care to translate? I want to know what you just called Ma." I know that it is flattering since both Mike and Elias have been her favorites for years.

"You mean there is a word that the bard of engine oil doesn't know?" Sheriff Rosewood is being sarcastic at my expense.

"It means magician and is the highest praise we have for a chef of such ability," Sheriff Wetherford replies.

"*Is-tee-hul-wah!*" I raise my mug—now almost empty—and am joined by all the others, even the uptight Tyler the third.

"I don't want to sound like a party pooper, but I think that we all have rather full agenda." Helen is always the voice of reason.

"I have a lot of protocols to put together," Dr. Hastings announces. "I will prepare a list of material I will need for COVID screening."

"Since we have implemented guidelines at TSA, I will immediately order for you what we would use at an airport with 100,000 people checking in for flights during a two hour window. I will assign experienced personnel for the entire week under your direction. We can go over details next week."

"Thank you, Mr. Douglas." The good doctor gives him her card. I know that it indicates that in addition to being a multiple board certified physician, she has a doctoral degree in Public Health. He seems duly impressed.

"Virgil and I have to prepare a couple of executive orders," Mayor Dixon adds.

"I am more than willing to offer the full weight of the Attorney General's office. We can prepare an opinion that your Orders are well within your respective mayoral author-ity to insure a safe environment for an event of international importance and in the interest of national security." Charles Stoddard doesn't say much, but when he does, it's pretty big time. "May I suggest that in addition to a no firearm order, attendees will be required to follow health and safety rules, which will definitely include taking temperatures and might even require masks if conditions warrant."

"I am more and more confidant that we will be able to pull this off." Olivia is clearly relieved there will be no unau-thorized weapons and health issues are being addressed.

"Dare I mention that we need to address both weapon and health issues for the Monday event?"

"That's touchy," Mr. Tsarkis answers. "Let me consider it a little more. I want to see how the G-7 meeting is being handled. I think it is unlikely that it can be very different from whatever has already been agreed upon. Drivers, crew, sponsors and owners will be subject to the same rules as will be applicable to the event itself. With the elimination of Formula-E from the program, we are reducing the pool of people by a third. I think we need to limit crew and groupies in both F-1 and vintage. This will only be an exhibition. The photo op will be far more important."

"We need to get final list of team members from all three race groups next week. There will be a lot of vetting and some hurt feelings when, not if, we make some cuts." I have the feeling that I should add that to my honey do list.

"I am satisfied that everything has been addressed. This is not to say that everything has been done, but again, I am relieved that we are working with a top notch professional team. May I suggest we get back to Washington? We each have a lot to do." Deputy Chief of Staff Tsarkis has spoken. So, let it be done. Everyone rises. Agent Forbes walks over to Sean and hands him an American Express card. Despite my initial foreboding, this group, with the exception of "the Third", is very classy.

Agent Forbes returns and asks Elias, "Do you need a lift?"

"Thanks, but I think Worth Avenue can survive without the Sheriff until tomorrow. We have a lot of logistics to go over. I'll take commercial in the morning."

We say our farewells. Olivia, Helen, the Boss, Mike, Elias, and I return to headquarters.

After about four hours of trying to identify and then resolve some of the logistic issues with which we are confronted, basically holding two races at two different venues in consecutive days we call it a day. Mike and Elias are heading off to a family dinner. Helen is going home to feed and walk her two pugs and Josh is going to coach a Little League game. That leaves Olivia and me.

We actually accomplished a lot. The current schedule is that the Formula One cars and the vintage open wheel pre 1960 cars, which even include Indy cars, will arrive at the Gold Coast track by 8 am on Monday. The Formula E cars will go directly to Orlando. Two speed modulated exhibition sessions for each class will begin at 10 and by 1 pm the cars will be off the track. A luncheon buffet is scheduled, followed by a photo op. Cars will be loaded and ready to head up I-95 toward Citrus Grove by 4:30 at the latest.

Tuesday is Media Day at the track and crews will use the time to get their cars tweaked for untimed practice Wednesday morning, followed by a timed practice for each group in the afternoon. Thursday F-1 and F-E will have two qualifying sessions, while the vintage cars will have two exhibition races. The vintage car drivers are usually also owners and are competing for fun. They have a format that requires the order the cars finish in the first race be reversed for the second race, so that the last place car is on the pole. Because of the disparity of driver ability and inherent speed of the cars, this gridding scenario could cause real havoc. But it doesn't. All the drivers are friends and therefore no one does anything stupid. If per chance a driver is too aggressive, he or she is black flagged during the race and sits in the pit for a lap or two. If it happens more than once, the driver is simply not asked to participate again. Anyway, the fans love it.

Friday is basically the same. Saturday, the F-1 cars have an untimed practice session since the grid has already been determined by the best time posted in qualifying. The vintage folks have a short race before lunch. The Formula E feature begins at 2 and is usually televised live. Since race engines are not permitted to be run until 11am Sunday, the vintage cars will have a short tour of the track and the F-1 feature and the corresponding pomp and ceremony will begin at noon. Thereafter Olivia and I take a two week holiday to an island without cell service.

CHAPTER SIX

As we exit the elevator in the parking garage, I turn to Olivia and say, "I really need a glass of wine and to watch the sunset with you." I give her a quick kiss on the cheek.

"And I need a shower, a glass of wine, and to stare at the moon with you. In case you weren't paying attention, the sun has already set."

"Sounds like a relaxing evening at home on the patio."

"Are you complaining?"

"Absolutely not . . . provided you leave me some hot water for my shower."

"I thought you wanted to take a shower together." Chief Detective returns my kiss on the cheek.

The journey back to Chez Nederfield/Ballard is much quicker, since all normal people have long since left their respective offices. "I may have to take a nap since I have several phone calls to make to folks in Europe. We have all cavalierly planned for the teams to come to Palm Beach, but we haven't asked them. Also, vetting is going to have to be so much more thorough, especially for the Palm Beach crowd."

"You really only have to worry about the F-1 and F-E folks since most of the vintage crowd will be either from the

U.S., Canada, or England. Their bona fides will be easier and faster to verify. We will need a list from the race organizers for all three race groups with as much information as possible, especially dates of birth, country of origin and passport number. I am glad that we are able to get the Feds to do the digging."

"We are probably talking about thirty different teams in each group and as many as ten crew members, a sponsor or two and an owner and a lot of camp followers. Bet there will be 400 or more warm bodies that we will have to keep track of."

"Put in those terms, I think we will need two glasses of wine." Olivia's smile lights up the encroaching dusk.

I rummage in the fridge and find enough ingredients to make an artichoke dip, which we spread on toasted pita bread. After lunch at Houlihan's, chips and dip and wine is perfect.

"Alexa, please turn on Frank Sinatra." I return to the patio with a tray, a smile, and great music.

"At your service."

The evening is exactly what the doctor ordered; peaceful and totally devoid of anything remotely cop related. I glance at my watch and am horrified to find that it is almost midnight.

"Olivia, I want to make a couple of calls to the U.K. Keep your fingers crossed." I dial. The makes that uniquely European ringing sound. On the fourth ring, it stops and a real human voice answers. "Sir Bertram please, it's Thomas Ballard."

I wait for about two minutes until an all too cheery voice comes on the phone. I push the speaker button. "Thomas, to what do I deserve an early morning call from a member of the fourth estate?"

"I have a favor to ask. A big favor. I have put the phone on speaker so Olivia could join us."

"You mean that vision of beauty is still putting up with you?"

"It is trying at times Sir Bertram, but I shall muddle on," Olivia replies.

"You will be pleased to know how hard she has been working to make the race safe and secure. Toward that end, we have to make a tiny adjustment to the program."

"As head of the FIA, I don't like adjustments with only six weeks to go, but knowing you, I don't think we would be having this call without good reason."

"Long and short; our President wants to host the members of the world community who will be attending the mini-G-7 meeting, as his guests at the F-1 race."

"You jest . . . don't you?"

"No sir. This bomb was dropped on us today. However, we think we can defuse most of the problem by staging an informal exhibition and meet and greet session on the Monday before race activities."

"That's possible since the previous weekend is open on our schedule. Adjust travel a bit. Hope your chaps can help with any added costs."

"That has already been agreed upon by the Deputy Chief of Staff."

"My, you are dealing with the big brass."

"There is a little bitty wrinkle," I say.

"Thomas, how little?"

"Well, we want to schedule the Monday event at the Gold Coast Raceway for F-1 and vintage only. The logistics of bringing these folks to Orlando would be a nightmare and a half. We already have our hands full with security and health issues at Citrus Grove. The further I can keep our President and all those dignitaries away from the race activities, the better."

"Agreed. How do you envision this working?"

"F-1 teams or at least some team members would drive their rigs from Orlando to Palm Beach in the morning. Drive around the track at a gentlemanly speed for a half hour. Attend a luncheon and head back up to Orlando late afternoon. The vintage would do the same."

"Not much room for error, is there?"

"No Sir Bertram, but it's the best we can come up with," Olivia adds.

"Let me suggest a slight variation to your plan. I get the F-1 folks to Central Florida on Saturday on the promise of a day at your wonderful Disney World or Universal." Sir Bertram laughs at his suggestion. "Since I suspect that the G-7 participants won't know the difference between a backup car and the actual race car, we can send the former to Palm Beach with a reduced crew since it will only be a warm up. The crews will have the number one car in a garage to do any last minute tuning. Save money and makes my sell to the teams a little easier."

"Which part? The backup car or Mickey Mouse?" We all laugh. "In order to entice the teams, I propose that the powers to be will make a substantial, like a very substantial, donation to the FIA Foundation," I add.

"Thomas, I understand that you are really against the wall. I remember being asked to stage a race before the Dubai G.P. for a Saudi Prince . . . and he wanted to race."

"How did you pull that off?" Detective Nederfield asks.

"Made sure that his car ran over a nail on the way to pit lane. I think his Highness was a bit put out, but there was nothing to be done."

"Well done. I didn't think you were that diabolical," I say.

"Moi? We British do not have a diabolical bone in our collective bodies . . . and I can make you a great deal on the London Bridge." Once again Sir Bertram has us laughing, as much from joy as from relief. I was very worried that this might not work and I didn't have a plan B.

"How do you suggest I approach the vintage folks?"

"Rather straightforward. The chap in charge is a rather fascinating character; a real live rocket scientist, a whiz bang mechanic, a very good driver, and quite pleasant. His name is Marshall Leventhal and divides his time between Washington State, Houston, and the Rolls Royce jet engine facility outside of London. He has two behemoth Alfa Romero's, a pre War 8C 35, which he keeps in the U.K. for European events, and the ex-Farina 158, which you will see. Easy bloke to talk to. I'll send you his contact information and drop him an email to expect to hear from you.

"Thank you Sir Bertram. You have made my life a lot easier."

"Olivia, my dear, get that poor boy to bed. It is far too late. Thomas, if you need any help, give me a ring."

"What I do need is the name, birth date, country of origin and passport number of anyone who is to be in the paddock and pits for both the real race and our "Dubai" race."

"Done, provided I get to the front of the line to see Harry Potter. Cheerio." Sir Bertram disconnects the call.

Olivia clears the table and says, "I think we should follow Sir Bertram's advice and get into bed."

"Before or after I take a shower?" I ask.

"Depends on whether you want to get into bed with me or sleep on the floor."

CHAPTER SEVEN

Both Olivia and I put our phones on mute, crawl into bed and immediately fall asleep. So much for a romantic evening. When I finally open my eyes, the sun has risen; Olivia has made a pot of coffee and is standing next to me waving the cup so that all the heavenly aroma fills my nostrils. I sit up and take a sip. Tastes as good as it smells; as it should.

"Good morning sunshine," she purrs. "It's after eight and our days are rather full. I have to go to the office and see whether everything else piled on my desk is being supervised. Then I want to drive over to the track and take a lot of pictures for my operations manual and then . . ."

"Meet me for a late lunch and watch a couple of modified races at New Smyrna. Despite what the Sheriff thinks, I do still work for a living. I'll write up a few paragraphs and post them on my blog so my millions of subscribers get their car fix for the day. I also want to track down Mr. Leventhal and get his gang on board."

"Since I'll be on the east side of the county, let's meet at the Blue Heron. I'm sure Lucy will let us leave a car in the lot until after the races."

I wiggle out of bed wearing nothing but my blue jammy bottoms. "Come here lovely lady." I reach out and give Detective Nederfield a hug and in the process stab myself on her badge which she is wearing on a chain. "Ouch!"

"Serves you right, you dirty old man."

"I took a shower last night." I lower my head.

"You are such a baby. Let me give you a kiss and make it better." She does. A very nice kiss indeed.

"See you a little before 2 for lunch," I say as Olivia opens the door.

"I'll bring the Ogre up to speed about the call with Sir Bertram. I am quite relieved. I'll tell him you'll be calling Deputy Chief of Staff Tsarkis with an update. He'll be happy he doesn't have to talk to one of the D.C. suits." Olivia leaves and I decide that a bowl of oatmeal with fresh blueberries and organic honey is the perfect breakfast. I wonder what Olivia ate. I opt not to drink another cup of coffee, but pour myself a large glass of fresh Florida orange juice, take my newspapers and oatmeal, and head out to the patio.

I realize that my leisurely morning has the possibility of becoming a day very wasted unless I get by butt in gear, figuratively speaking. In addition to reaching out to Marshall Leventhal, I have to do some research for today's super modified race, write a few pithy paragraphs for my faithful followers, and call Nicholas Tsarkis. Another shower is definitely the next thing on the agenda. It is a great relief that I finally broke down and hired someone to cut the lawn and trim the hedges. I like gardening, but mowing just doesn't excite me, except that I love the smell almost as much as Castrol.

I opt to defer the shower for a quick email to the vintage formula car director, since I may have to wait for a reply. I hope Sir Bertram has given him the lay of the land.

"*Good morning,*" I type. "*My name is Thomas Ballard and in addition to being a journalist, I am a deputy sheriff here in Central Florida and have been assigned the duty, or rather the pleasure, of being one of the point persons for the upcoming event at Citrus Grove. I hope Sir Bertram has spoken to you so that this is not coming out of the blue. If you can spare a few minutes, I would like to go over some details regarding the race. Please email me with a number I can call and time we can chat. I am on the right hand coast which will allow you to calculate time zone issues. Thanks.*"

For some people a shower is a great place to sing. For me it is a great place to think, especially with extra hot water pounding the back of my neck. My thoughts for today are filled with *how are we ever going to keep the Monday event a relative secret?* Maybe it isn't worth the effort. Putting a lid on the F-1 folks would be hard enough. The vintage folks are probably easier. But the White House has more leaks than a colander. I hope that Elias has a contract for the Gold Coast track in hand. Wait until I drop our plans on its owner. Charles Shaw is not the easiest or most pleasant person to deal with, but deal with him I must. Zillions of cops, FBI agents, Secret Service personnel, limos filled with diplomats each sporting the flag of the country of their occupants and a couple of helicopters might indicate that this is more than a law enforcement driver's school. And then there's the press. I'm going to let Tsarkis tell me who he wants in attendance and let him vet them. Same with personal security people that might be with the diplomats. I would feel better if I can get a green light on a no firearms order except for our guys. Let him use the same protocol as is being used for the mini summit. And we need a no fly zone around the track.

The water is beginning to get cold, indicating that I should turn off the shower and stop thinking. I definitely have to post something for my adoring fans, so thinking is out of the question for a while. Slightly fades jeans, a beige fishing shirt, and deck shoes will be the day's attire. Casual, oh so Florida and comfortable.

Since the F-1 race is still in the planning stage, I want to entertain my readers with more mundane things like a very cool classic four car race last weekend on the two car wide oval at Bristol with some very important points at stake. The weather was clear and hot and the track was dry and sticky. Two Fords (teammates) one Chevy and a battle scared Toyota circled the track about an inch apart bringing back memories of some old school racing. Since the track is shorter than most championship courses, the speeds are substantially lower and aerodynamics plays less of a role than at the superspeedways. I try to attend most east coast NASCAR races during the season and although I should maintain journalistic objectivity, both Olivia and I cheer for Don Montgomery in his Camaro, who is in his first full year with a great team, of which I am the overseer, as distinguished from the owner. I am pleased that Don's decisions are calculated upon the probability that the result will be beneficial to him. As an engineer, he appreciates his machine and the importance of finishing a race, preferably close to the front.

At Bristol, being a quarter of a lap behind the leaders leaves barely enough room to steer around the inevitable carnage which awaits. The *big one,* as we refer to crashes which occur with painful regularity, took place eight laps before the checker. The Camry, which had already tangled with several cars earlier in the race, tired to shorten his travel time by racing below the inside yellow line. One of the Mustangs took offense even before the starter could wave the black flag, and drove the Toyota into the bottom Safeco wall. What driver's call the red mist or red haze must have clouded whatever judgment the Toyota driver still had because he drove up the track from the bottom and took out all three remaining leading competitors, which left the red, green, and white number 31 Camaro, piloted by rookie Montgomery to avoid the bits and pieces of wreckage and take the lead just as the yellow flag came out. Although it was a mess, the officials felt that there was enough clean track for the race to continue under caution. And thus it ended with our driver winning his first trophy event. I need another shower after writing the piece. I feel like I was sitting in the sweltering heat of a race car. But alas, my cell phone vibrates to tell me I have an email. Think about that; one device advises you that another device has a message. I guess I could read it on by 4.7 inch cell screen, but it is not something I enjoy if I can avoid it. *If you are free in ten minutes, please call me at 888-644-6601. Marshall.*

I think the best way to approach this is straight on. Tell Mr. Leventhal exactly what's up. It worked with Sir Bertram, so I am going to stick with it. I get a Dr. Pepper from the fridge and dial.

"Good morning, my name is Thomas Ballard and I want to ask for your help in planning an exhibition event on the Monday preceding the Formula race at Citrus Grove. May I put you on speaker so I can write notes?"

"Until last night, I thought you were simply a world renown automotive journalist," Marshall Leventhal's baritone voice booms through the speaker. "I learned from Sir Bertram that you are also a member of law enforcement and based on certain, shall I say requests from 1600 Pennsylvania

Avenue; you are also an event planner and juggler." I hear a chortle in the background.

"That about sums it up. I need some of the vintage participants to put on a show for POTUS and his guests. I decided that bringing the show to Gold Coast Raceway was going to be a lot easier logistically than bringing seven world leaders to Citrus Grove."

"I don't envy your job. Between security and health considerations, planning must be a nightmare. We can surely get at least some of the cars to Palm Beach on Monday and put on a dog and pony show."

"If you can canvas your members and see who can come, I will need their names, addresses, passport numbers or driver's license numbers. The Secret Service has to vet the drivers and their crew and I want to get that done as soon as possible. We are only six weeks out." I hope I don't sound like I'm whining.

"I have a list of entrants and email addresses and will send out a blast today. I will provide as little information as possible, since I suspect that this could become a media feeding frenzy."

"Thank you for understanding. My only other choice was for the entire G-7 mini conference to ascend upon us all on race day with a hundred-thousand folks in attendance. That would have been a Force Five debacle. I look forward to getting the list as soon as possible. I have no idea how long it will take the boys in D.C. to run the names."

"I look forward to meeting you in Palm Beach and beyond. Later." Marshall Leventhal ends the call.

I still have to put in a call to Elias Rosewood before I meet Olivia. I have a feeling that we may have to visit Mr. Shaw at his track to tell him what to expect and between Olivia and Elias; I think we can get his attention.

CHAPTER EIGHT

The Blue Heron is only about thirty minutes from the house and so I still have another hour to call Sheriff Rosewood and Deputy Chief of Staff Tsarkis. I choose the latter first since I have little to say, but sense that the suits like to be in the loop regardless of whether it is empty or not. I have already programmed my phone with his number so I simply speed dial.

"Good morning Mr. Tsarkis. Thomas Ballard here," I announce after reaching him directly. "I wanted to bring you up to date. I have talked with both the head of the F-1 contingent, Sir Bertram Hollingsworth, and of the vintage group, Marshall Leventhal." I pause.

"Yes, the rocket scientist. Both have agreed to take the necessary steps to make sure the G-7 crowd is entertained. I asked them each to give me a roster of participants so that you all can run background checks. Hopefully, I can send them along sometime tomorrow to you with a copy to Kent Forbes and Dan Driver. Since time is of the essence, please assign sufficient resources to the vetting so that I can call Marshall and Sir Bertram no later than Monday. I'm meeting with Chief Detective Nederfield in about an hour to go over security at Citrus Grove and then we may meet Sheriff Rosewood in Palm Beach." I again pause.

"Thank you. We aim to please. Oh, I need a list of media attendees for the exhibition. I do not want to be involved in either selection or clearance. My plate is full. I will send each of them the standard media protocol form I am using for the weekend races. There will be no exceptions. If anything untoward comes up, I will let you know. I am sure Sheriff Rosewood is going to want a procedure for submitting expenses. I think his budget did not contemplate a presidential visit to a track he has had to rent." I hang up. I am glad Nicholas Tsarkis is a man of few words.

Next up, Elias. I assume the Sheriff of Palm Beach County is otherwise engaged out of the office, so I figure I'll leave a message. He can call this afternoon and we can arrange a get together with Charles Shaw tomorrow. I want to leave as few things to chance as possible. An iced tea for the road and I'm ready to face the world after I go through my check list: turn up the A/C since there is no point in cooling an empty house; grab my lap top; and set the alarm. Olivia drove to Citrus Grove in a motor pool Explorer, so I decide to enjoy the ride in the VW with the top down. It's more economical than the F-250 and since our mileage reimbursement is a flat $.55/mile and the beetle gets 26 miles/gallon and gas costs a little less than two bucks, I make a modest profit. That's total BS. I just like to drive a convertible on a Chamber of Commerce day in Central Florida.

Times have really changed. It used to be that seeing an Explorer, Expedition or F-150 (or the Chevrolet or Dodge equivalents) in the parking lot of a somewhat upscale restaurant at 2 in the afternoon would be rare. I have to search for Olivia's motor pool mount for five minutes. Since there are no light bars or markings on the gray Explorer, it looks like twenty other vehicles. I park the VW as close as I dare. SUV doors are by nature wide and heavy, so I leave plenty of room. Olivia would be a mite upset if even the littlest blemish found its way onto her pride and joy. I decide to raise the top and roll up the windows in case one of Orange County's infamous afternoon thunder storms should befall us while at lunch.

The always gorgeous Chief Detective Nederfield is already seated at a corner table for six, anticipating we might need to spread out and examine some papers. "I ordered you an unsweetened iced tea," Olivia purrs. "The crab dip is today's special appetizer and I am assured that one order with some soup would be more than enough food for a big time special deputy."

"Sounds perfect. Let's order. I want to hear about your day and fill you in on what I have been doing."

Right on cue, the server appears with our drinks. "We are going to share the crab dip and each have a cup of conch chowder. Thanks."

"I decided to give the Beetle some exercise," I begin.

"I assumed you would once I saw how nice the weather was."

"Who was at the meeting?" I ask.

"Mike was there along with a State Police superinten-dent, a couple of knuckleheads from Tallahassee on behalf of the governor, Bill Blaney, he's one of the track owners, Terry McAlister from the regional FBI office and Sheila White," Olivia replies.

"Who is Sheila White?" I have never heard her name in connection with law enforcement.

"She is the new head of TSA. Really tech savvy. She will be of tremendous help with screening not only at Citrus Grove, but at Palm Beach as well. She has been given instructions from Nicholas Tsarkis to give us anything we need. She has a counterpart at ATF who will be handling the canine cops. Some of the gadgets can be used on Monday, disassembled and moved up here in a matter of hours. Homeland Security will provide experienced operators, who will be notified of their assignments less than 24 hours before the respective events. Remember: *loose lips sink ships*."

I am glad our food has arrived. I am starved and I am not sure how many homilies I can handle?

Lunch was as advertised—excellent. A glass of Pinot Grigio might have been warranted, but we still have a lot to do. "Where do you see problems?" I ask.

"I think we have the perimeter pretty well under control. With the no weapons Executive Order, I feel pretty good. The teams will have to be brought up to date regarding both health and security measures. Needless to say, I would feel better if a mandatory mask order would be in effect, but it isn't going to happen. Temperature checks is the best we'll be able to do."

"Do you have any thoughts about paddock accessibility? I would prefer that only team members and approved media are in the infield. The camping crowd can be assigned to the outside paddocks at the far ends of the track. Plenty of bathrooms." I chuckle, but only slightly. The dyed in the wool fans consume a lot of beer during almost five days of racing and most will need showers with hot water at least once during the event.

"Law enforcement presence will be obvious enough to deter most bad behavior. I actually thought about reducing the numbers of uniformed personnel until Mike said that *an ounce of prevention is worth a pound of cure.*" More homilies.

"A lot of the spectators will have attended Formula 1 events in other countries where members of the military armed with automatic weapons walk around both outside and inside the venue. People are getting accustomed to the new normal." It's a sign of the times.

"Thomas, the Palm Beach event poses far more issues, including a lot of folks who don't like being told what to do and where to go," Olivia proffers.

"That's why, my dear, we may have to go to Gold Coast Raceway with Elias and his team. I think that Dan, the guy from the Bureau and Sheila White should join us. I am waiting for a call back from the good Sheriff Rosewood. We have a lot of unknowns." Suddenly my pocket vibrates. I usually do not look at, let alone answer, my cell while dining, but this is a working lunch. It's an email from Marshall Leventhal: "*Most of the info you wanted was in our data base so I thought you would want to get started. See attached. Am asking each team to confirm ASAP. Marshall.*" Rather than read the email, I hand Olivia my phone. "I'm going to forward this to Tsarkis. He can pass it on to whomever." Olivia returns my phone and I send the message on its way to D.C.

"Mr. Leventhal is quite efficient," Chief Detective Nederfield observes.

"Hey, he's a rocket scientist," I quip. "Let's go for a ride and try to find a farm stand before we head over to New Smyrna for the modified races."

"Good idea. I drive . . . my car. There are a couple of places I read about that sell fantastic berries and melons."

I rise and like the polite young man my mother made me and gently pull back Olivia's chair for which I get a kiss on the cheek. We leave arm in arm.

Again my phone vibrates. The caller ID says *PBC Sheriff.* "It's Elias," I whisper. Olivia nods and I answer. "Good afternoon great warrior. I am putting you on speaker so that Chief Detective Nederfield can hear."

"Are you still hanging around with that writer?" Elias asks.

"Actually he is hanging around with me. Like a lost little puppy." That brings gales of laughter.

"I hate to break up this little chit chat, but do you have the track rental agreement in hand?"

"In fact I have a fully signed document giving us full and exclusive use of Gold Coast Raceway from 6 in the morning until 6 in the evening. We supply all fire and safety equipment and personnel. The lease says *Track Day*, on the use line. So we are home free. Well not exactly free. Shaw charged the County $5,000 rental fee, which we paid by check this morning."

"You are a gentleman and a scholar. I spoke with Nicholas Tsarkis and he is setting up an account to reimburse you all. Every cop on duty that day gets time and a half for a twelve hour day, as well as regular duty time for setting up, all compliments of POTUS. Olivia wants to round up some folks and if schedules work, meet you tomorrow with your team at the track around 10:30 so we miss traffic on the Turnpike. I will have to bite the bullet and tell Charles Shaw to meet us and let him in on our plans. If he blabs, promise me you will have him disappear into the 'Glades, never to return."

"Can I cut out his tongue as well?"

"That's what I like about working with you and Mike. No screwing around. Get right to the point." We both laugh.

"We'll meet you at the track. I'll bring some water and soda on ice and you bring coffee and donuts since you probably know the best donut shop in South Florida."

"I get no respect, but I do know a place to die for . . . figuratively speaking. *Tchah* Thomas."

"*Hi-e-pas eyaha*" I hang up.

"I thought you didn't speak Seminole." Olivia seems surprise at my erudition.

"Only a smattering." I get a dirty look from Olivia. "Hey, it's Elias' name . . . Little Wolf."

"Thomas, I think I had better rain check the race. I've got to call several people about tomorrow."

"If I happen to pass a stand on the way home I'll pick up some veggies and make my famous stir fry on the griddle. Deal?"

"Yes dear. And don't put a scratch on the Explorer. Motor pool will be cross." Olivia tosses me the keys to the unmarked Orange County Sheriff's vehicle and saunters off to her adorable VW."

CHAPTER NINE

You can see the oval at New Smyrna from Route 44. It gives me that same *warm all over feeling* that I get coming upon a drive-in movie theater. So old school. I am glad that lower echelon stock car racing hasn't yet been priced out of the reach for the younger set. Tee shirts and jeans are the fashion of the day for both men and women. That's one of the differences between now and then. Both my parents loved car racing and as a family we would go all over the state together. Mom was one of a handful of women in attendance, except for the so-called *beauty queens* who would adorn cars and drivers, and I, as a young child, was definitely a rarity. Now racing has become a family, often multi-generational sport and I am glad. There is nothing cuter than a five year old wearing ear protection walking around the paddock examining his dad's or sometimes mom's competition. A cold beer never tasted better than at a race track. And the hot dogs are incomparable. The racing is pretty good, too. Modifieds are barely recognizable from their origins, mostly as soccer-mobiles. The engines are unmuffled and sometimes it feels like an earthquake, but I love it. Race gas and race oil-it doesn't get any better than this. The lower classes of stockcar racing are fun to watch—no pretension—just peddle to the metal.

Normally Olivia joins me, and several of the wives or girlfriends of the male drivers have bonded with her. Not only is she a commanding presence at 6'2", but she willing to help tune a carb or change a tire. In part because she is knowledgeable and in part because she is a cop. Domestic violence is an insidious and often hidden secret in families and I think knowing that a member of law enforcement is readily accessible tends to shine a light into the dark corners. Olivia is a serious cog in local racing and it is obvious when several women ask about her. I assure them that she spent the morning at Citrus Grove, but she had to get back to the office. They understand balancing cars and jobs. They are all good after I tell them we are going to attend Saturday's event at the Fairgrounds.

I leave before the feature races so I can get home before dark and maybe snag some veggies along the way. Although I am in major avoidance mode about confronting Charlie Shaw, I email him that Elias and I would be at the track at 10:30 tomorrow and hoped he had a few minutes. I decided that I would tell him a little white lie that the Sheriff's office, in addition to practicing driving, would be carrying on a drill that included providing security for very important people at large public venues. Since I am reasonable certain he has read my articles, I thought it made for a better cover story than the truth. He couldn't handle the truth anyway. I speed dial Olivia's cell.

I go immediately into voice mail. "Hi darling. I am on the way home with a large bag of fresh produce, includ-ing some baby spinach for a salad with mixed berries and a vinaigrette. I also have a baguette of freshly baked multi grain bread. Are you home yet?"

Driving a Sheriff's vehicle, especially an unmarked one, gives you a certain sense of power which must be controlled at all costs regardless of the temptation to turn on the emergency lights and maybe the siren when some jerk cuts you off. There once was a county tax collector who had blue lights installed in his personal Escalade and would pull people over for speeding or lane changing without signaling. And he wore his tax collector's badge, which looked a lot like my deputy's badge, on a chain around his neck. He was indicted and removed from office. Florida politics as usual.

My cell vibrates. "Thomas Ballard here." I hadn't checked the caller ID to see that it was Olivia. "Agreed! First one home gets to use the shower provided said first one puts a bottle of Chardonnay in the refrigerator." She giggles when we end. I'll bet she's in the driveway, poised to use up the hot water once again.

My return trip takes about forty five minutes, so I am reconciled to cold water, but a great salad. Since the VW lays claim to the garage, I ease the Explorer behind my bright red F-250. People have asked me why I bought a red vehicle in Florida. The sun always fades the paint to a pale pink, they say. That's because they don't know Ken the body man, who for $50, will clay bar and wax the truck. It's six years old and gets a beauty treatment every four months or so and looks like new. Ha!

"I'm home," I announce.

"I left you some hot water," Olivia replies from the bedroom. "And I picked up a nice Rosé from Province which is chilling in a bucket."

"You are a classy lady."

"I know. Wait until I tell you about my phone calls. Get clean."

I don't wait to be told a second time. I decide against leaving a trail of clothes on the way to the bathroom although it would be a funny movie visual. I get yelled at for leaving a mess. Even as a spectator, a film of dirt always covers you after attending a car race and the remaining hot water feels great. I wrap a towel around my private parts and head to the bedroom with an armful of clothes for the hamper. Olivia is standing at the kitchen sink.

"Everything you bought looks and smells so fresh. You should write down where the farm stand is so we can go back again."

"It's right on 415 near Enterprise. I put the GPS coordinates in my phone already."

"What an enterprising young man you are." Olivia starts to laugh at her own joke.

"While you're standing there smelling the goods, what about washing everything?"

"I have a colander at the ready. Go get dressed and we can sit on the patio before it gets dark."

I return in my favorite post shower ensemble—baggy shorts and a light weight fishing shirt. "May I open a bottle of vino for m'lady?"

"But of course, kind sir. The glasses are chilled."

I swiftly attend to my sommelier duties and we retire to the patio to watch the last rays of sun dip below the western horizon. Life is good.

"What news do you bring?" We may be overdoing the medieval thing a bit.

"Nicholas Tsarkis is very good at his job and true to his word. Everyone has been rounded up for tomorrow. We are meeting at 8:30 at the Executive Airport and are being flown to Palm Beach in a government jet."

"No wonder our taxes are high. I better call Elias and tell him about the change of plans."

"Done. He will pick us up in a van and we will all go together to the track. His folks will be there as planned at 10:30." I have visions of Elias picking us up in a paddy wagon as a joke. "Did you reach Shaw?"

"I emailed him. I haven't looked to see if he has replied. When we go back in for dinner, I'll check the computer."

"I talked with Josh at the office and he is pleased we have everything in hand. The County budget is due next week and he is having apoplexy. Mike is happy his cousin is on board and he's confident that Elias will more than hold up his end."

"I'll drink to that." I raise my glass and lean over to give Olivia a kiss which she returns in kind. "Let's head inside." I still want to perfect my little white lie and check email.

CHAPTER TEN

I quickly check my emails, some from my worldwide cadre of followers. My article about the race at Bristol was well received, thank goodness. Several asked if I could do a piece on the rising young NASCAR star, Don Montgomery. I chuckle and decide to forward the comment to him.

"Olivia, I think we should do something special for Don to commemorate his first Tournament Cup win. They're racing at Atlanta this weekend and we could hop up on Sunday. We have to be at the Fairgrounds on Saturday and I am pretty sure the folks from Kim Tires will be there. I'll check. I bet we can hitch a ride on their corporate plane to Atlanta and fly commercial after the race and hopefully dinner with Don."

"Sounds like a plan," she shouts from the kitchen. "Everything is ready for your culinary expertise."

"I just want to go through the rest of my emails."

I skip over the non-time sensitive communications and open a missive from Palm Beach Raceway. *See you at 10:30. Charles.* Great, now I have more time to come up with my smokescreen.

I scroll down and notice an email from Sir Bertram. *Thomas, attached is the information you requested. I sent the list to a friend who is very wired at Interpol, as well. I wanted quick and efficient initial vetting, although I am sure other venues have done background checks. Let me know what else I can do. Cheerio.*

I reply, *Thanks. I am sending to Nicholas Tsarkis, deputy chief of Staff for POTUS and am copying you so you have his contact info. We are going to the Palm Beach track tomorrow with folks to set up the event. I'll keep you in the loop. Thanks again.* I hit *send* and then forward Sir Bertram's email and list to Nicholas. Time for dinner.

I decide to warm the spinach in a frying pan with a dollop of turkey bacon renderings, and then place the warm greens onto a plate, adding the blueberries, raspberries and blackberries Olivia has just washed. The bread is so fresh I elect not to heat it. I put some olive oil with fresh basil into a dish for dunking the sliced bread and we are ready to eat. I add a splash of Vidalia onion vinaigrette to the salad and place the plates on the table, pull back Olivia's chair for ease of access and say "Alexa, play Stan Getz."

Needless to say, dinner is terrific and there are no leftovers.

"Thomas, I'll clean up while you send the folks at Kim Tires a note regarding the race at Atlanta. I have been thinking of getting Don something special. Try and find a wire service photo of him crossing the finish line with the checkered flag. I have an idea."

"I'll only be a minute," I return to my computer which is anxiously flashing that I have an important email. It's from Nicholas Tsarkis. *Please call.* It was sent only about twenty minutes ago so I assume he means now. "Olivia, I got an email from Tsarkis I want you to see."

"You sound concerned, what is it?" The Chief Detective of the Orange County Sheriff's office enters the office room, drying her hands on a Snoopy dish towel I have had since forever.

"He wants me to call him. He sent the email less than a half hour ago. Do you think he means . . . now?"

"It's only 9:30. Better to err on the safe side and give him a call. You have his cell number and if he is busy, he won't answer."

"Good point." I dial.

"Thomas thanks for getting back to me so promptly. If Detective Nederfield is with you, put me on speaker so that you won't have to repeat what I am about to tell you."

I do.

"Good evening," Olivia purrs.

"I just got back the preliminary report from the FBI regarding the backgrounds of the vintage formula drivers. Other than to say that this is a very impressive group, I got back reports on eight participants that are very disturbing. The eight apparently belong to one team which has entered two cars. Next to each of the names, rather than the basic background information, it simply says *don't ask*."

Olivia and I cannot contain ourselves and although rude, we start to loudly laugh.

"I'm sorry, but I bet I can give you the names of the seven men and one woman," I half choke and half speak.

"How did you know there was one woman?" The Deputy Chief of Staff sputters.

Olivia, who is somewhat more composed than I am, says, "Margaret Leiter is a very good friend of ours, as is her husband Hans and brother Pierre. The remaining five, Franco, Frederick, Stanford, Charles Llewellyn and his brother Cecil definitely all fall into the *don't ask* category, but we can give you the names of some folks who will vouch for their bona fides, including the Chairman of the Joint Chiefs. They are the most wonderful and resourceful folks and we feel relieved that they will be in attendance. There is not a law enforcement or national security agency they cannot access."

"I am relieved, but I still need to vet them." Nicholas Tsarkis is really upset.

"We can send you a list of names for you to contact. I am sure you will be satisfied, although I expect you will get a lot of *don't ask* replies. It's still early enough to call General Cramer at the Pentagon. Do you have his cell number? I have it if you don't. Ask him about these folks."

"How do you have General Cramer's cell number?"

"Don't ask," we answer in unison.

"I may have underestimated you two."

"We are but humble servants," I reply. "But never underestimate the Bentley Seven, plus one."

"This is highly irregular, but I will make inquiry of several people with whom I have confidence and get back to you tomorrow around ten-ish. I understand you will be meeting with resources on the ground to go over the venue."

"I am sorry if we have upset you Deputy Chief of Staff, but we have worked with these people and know that they can deliver the goods." I hope I don't sound too dramatic.

"Tomorrow at 10." The call is ended.

"I'm not sure that went all that well," Olivia remarks.

"He'll figure it out. His type doesn't like it when other people know things that he doesn't know. Once he gets a few *don't ask* replies, he'll be on board. We've got a full day tomorrow so let's get some shut eye."

"You mean the great Thomas Ballard is tired?"

"Yes, your highness and aren't you thrilled?" I get up and give Olivia a kiss and whisper, "I get the bathroom first" and sprint to the door.

"You are a creep . . . but I love you anyway."

CHAPTER ELEVEN

The morning comes early because Olivia wants us to put in a few miles, as she says, before we head out to the executive airport, which is only about fifteen minutes from our house and has ample parking. I hate being a slave to the computer, but I need to see if Kim Tires had gotten back to me. I really want to be with the crew of #31 Camaro and their up and coming driver. It's a bit complicated, but as far as NASCAR is concerned, I am the team owner. After the prior owner was no longer in a position to actively run the team, he gave it to me to take care of, together with enough money for the remainder of last year's season. I am not in the same economic league as other owners and I really thought that young Donald should ultimately be an owner as well as a driver; I started to look for sponsors. Once certain members of the *family* up in Providence realized that Cosmo's nephew could be the next Italian-American motorsports super star and having an uncle who had been made and was killed in the line of duty, our team suddenly became credible and competitive. *Tessa Pizza* may not be a household name, but with over eight hundred locations throughout the country, albeit most in New England, it has no problem writing checks. Don's management style was also very frugal. Since the tire limitations for the lower divisions are less restrictive and because of our close relationship with the Kim Family, we found our fortunes soaring. Don is turning out to be a very conscientious owner/driver. His engineering background made him very attentive to details and as a result in his first full season at the Trophy level, he has finished every race in the top 10, and the Bristol victory vaulted him into playoff contention. He is also the point leader for the so-called junior level class in a car shod with Kim Tires. It is funny to see his face in an ad for Kim Tires with text in Korean.

"Thomas, are you ready?" Detective Nederfield is wearing a jogging outfit that could cause male coronary arrest along our route.

"Five minutes," I shout.

I must be a very important person. I have an email from Jung Kim himself, vice president of Kim Enterprises and chief operating officer of the tire division and also a member of an elite Korean intelligence unit. But that's another story. *We would love to provide transport for you and the lovely Miss Olivia to Atlanta. We have several motor homes and will have a room for you each way. More reliable than plane and food is better.* He adds an emoji of a smiling face.

"Here I come ready or not!" I shout.

"Promises, promises." Olivia is stretching in the living room.

"I got an email from Jung Kim. He's offered us a ride in his RV both ways. I figure that we have a ten hour drive, so we will arrive in plenty of time and in style."

"Great but now it's time to shake a tail feather."

I set the house alarm and we start our morning run. Fortunately, we pace ourselves since I didn't do any stretching.

Three miles goes by very quickly. The sidewalk width or rather lack thereof, requires us to run in single file. She leads, I follow. I enjoy the view.

Since the Sheriff's Explorer is still in the driveway, we elect to use it to go to the airport. There's plenty of parking, but it is open and the VW is very upset if it gets wet from one of our frequent afternoon showers. We park next to a gray Crown Victoria with government plates, another Explorer, also with government plates and a beat up pickup truck. The latter obviously does not belong to someone in our party. I am introduced to Sheila White and am immediately impressed. No nonsense, but with a smile. We board, buckle up, and suddenly we are hot footing it down to Palm Beach. I guess I won't be getting a Bloody Mary.

I could get used to private jets. In less than forty minutes we are on the ground being greeted by Elias Rosewood and a female deputy who is every bit as tall as Olivia.

"Good morning. I want you to meet Deputy Rachael Silver. She is a former Navy Intel officer, specializing in counter terrorism. Although there is not a lot of that here in Palm Beach County, Rachael has been invaluable at looking at places and people and seeing things we all take for granted. I trust her judgment and her instinct completely. Maybe because we were both taught by the same expert *people reader*, our mother. Palm Beach County extends from the beaches of the Atlantic and Worth Avenue to the edge of the 'Glades and Lake Okeechobee. The people and the typography are varied, as are the issues confronting them. Nepotism in the department is usually discouraged but since I have run unopposed for sheriff for sixteen years, I'm not going to worry. If anyone can spot a bad apple, it's my little sister." The latter comment is made tongue in cheek.

"I am honored to join this illustrious group and will hold up my end." Everyone nods.

"Shall we pile into the County's finest limo and head over to the track?" Elias gestures toward to fifteen passenger white van with green lettering which says, *Palm Beach County Sheriff* and has metal mesh screening on the windows. In compliance with CDC guidelines, the van is sterilized after every use . . . more or less." Sheriff Rosewood laughs at his own joke.

It smells like disinfectant, which is a good thing. We set out for the track after buckling our seat belts. Without warning, Sheila White begins to sing, *100 bottles of beer on the wall*. Everyone's funny bone is tickled and we all join in, even FBI Agent Forbes.

We are having way too much fun, but the singing seems to create a kind of bonding, which is good. I dread having to deal with track owner Shaw, but by the time we reach *77 bottles of beer,* we are at the front entrance and being met by a pair of uniforms in cruisers.

"Thomas," Elias shouts. "FYI, Shaw is no longer the owner of the track. Apparently he ran into some financial trouble last year when the entire season was cancelled and has sold out to a huge Korean conglomerate. They want to use the track as a testing facility for their tire division."

Olivia and I just look at each other with open mouths from which we utter, "Kim Tire?"

"Yes. How did you know? It's very hush, hush. Even you snoopy journalist types aren't supposed to know."

"Elias, don't drive for a minute. Folks, I've got to tell you something real important and quite frankly something that makes me breathe a lot easier about using this venue."

"Pray tell," Sheila White says.

"What I am about to say cannot leave this vehicle. Period. At some point, we may want to widen our scope of those in the know, but not until I make some calls. Agreed?"

Everyone nods but I sense Secret Service Agent Driver may have his fingers crossed behind his back.

"Detective Nederfield is less long winded than I am, so please give everyone the short version."

"Jung Kim is the chief operating officer of the tire division of Kim Enterprises, of which he is a vice president and which his family owns. It is one of the world's largest high tech companies. Jung is someone we know very well. In fact we will be with him this weekend. He is also a very major player in the Korean Intelligence Bureau. Thomas and I worked with him on an international drug case last year with extremely favorable results. He also provides tires to a race team we are involved with. I want to bring him into the planning of this event. It's his track and with his help and understanding of what we are trying to do, the logistics will be a zillion times easier."

"I know that both Agents Forbes and Driver are squirming right now because what we are saying is above their place in the Federal hierarchy. It's not above mine. May I make a simple inquiry, by email, to a colleague and confirm Mr. Kim's bona fides?" Sheila White is a take charge kind of person. No wonder Olivia likes her.

Suddenly my phone starts to ring. "Shit," I mutter a little too loud, which gets everyone's attention. It's Nicholas Tsarkis. Thomas Ballard here, I am putting you on speaker with Detective Nederfield, Ms. White, Agents Forbes and Driver, and Sheriff Rosewood and his deputy. We are in a secure place."

"I have done some digging regarding the individuals about whom we spoke last night. I am not happy, but I am 100% comfortable. I have never been given such a complete brush off regarding national security by so many all saying the same thing: *don't ask*. I even threatened having the President intervene. No one blinked. I don't know who these friends of yours are, but they are thought of so highly by so many, I have no choice but to green light their attendance. I'm not sure I could red light their attendance at the event."

"Thank you Deputy Chief of Staff for your vote of confidence. I have another Maalox moment for you. The track in Palm Beach is now owned by Kim Enterprises. They bought it last year for product testing so there is no connection between our event and their ownership. I want your permission to include Jung Kim, who is the head of the division of Kim Enterprises which bought the track."

"What?" Nicholas Tsarkis shows quite a bit of emotion.

"Please let me finish. Mr. Kim is a member of the South Korean Intelligence community and Detective Nederfield and I have previously worked with him on a rather large drug investigation. He is not only trustworthy, he is knowledgeable and our effort to get the track secure will be handled discretely without any potential leak." It's sometimes hard to talk to D.C. types.

"Excuse me, Sheila White speaking. I have just confirmed Mr. Kim's identity with a colleague of mine and Homeland Security is satisfied that if we can bring Mr. Kim into our planning group, it will be very beneficial. Without belaboring this call, Deputy Ballard and Detective Nederfield will be with Mr. Kim over the weekend unrelated to the event and I think they should pitch him on helping us."

"This is all rather irregular." Tsarkis is still sputtering. "Based on my due diligence regarding some of Detective Nederfield and Deputy Ballard friends, I am quite impressed. If you all think it is the right course to take, do so."

"Thank you and we will keep you informed. I hang up and say, "I am in awe of Ms. White."

The TSA head holds up her phone. "I only heard back a few seconds ago from my colleague about Kim. I had to stop Tsarkis' driveling. He's sitting in a huge office in the White House and we're sitting in a prisoner's van in steamy Florida with a lot of work to do which can be facilitated by Mr. Kim's help."

I try not to cheer. "Giddy up *eyaha*! You heard the lady; we've got a lot of work to do."

Deputy Silver looks at her brother.

"Hey, he's Mike's friend. Don't blame me."

I look at Olivia, who is trying to stifle a laugh. "Deputy Rachael Silver is a bit off put by my grasp of her native tongue." I whisper.

"No, she now knows what we all know."

I raise one eyebrow. "And what do we all know?"

"You can be a bit over the top." She leans over and gives me a kiss.

"Hey, no fraternizing in the back of the van," Elias shouts.

"*Let-kus chatolaswa*," I reply.

Once again Olivia stares at me.

"Touché," Sheriff Rosewood answers. His sister has her mouth open, but nothing is said.

"You two sound like code whisperers," Sheila White announces.

"Kind of," Elias and I respond together.

CHAPTER TWELVE

Waiting our arrival, dressed in a white linen suit with a Panama hat, is none other than Charles *pain in the butt* Shaw. Who wears a white suit at a race track? I brace myself for the phony British accent.

"Thomas old sport, good to see you again. Here to help our local constabulary with their preparations?"

"Actually Charles, we have something a lot bigger in mind and I have checked with Jung Kim and he's on board."

The former race track impresario turns bright red. "How do you know?"

"Lest you forget I am an automotive journalist with investigative instincts. We have everything under control and I hope you weren't inconvenienced by being dragged out to the track? Have you met Sheriff Rosewood whose county coffers are now five thousand dollars less than they should be? Can you help him out, Charles?"

After a great deal of internal hemming and hawing, Shaw mumbles something to the effect that the check is in his office and he will go over and fetch it. I nod in assent.

"Nicely done Deputy Ballard," Sheila White says.

"Thanks." That's all I can think of to say since I want to email Jung Kim with a head's up in case Shaw tries to check up on me. "Something very important has come up and it involves your Palm Beach race track. I'll explain when I see you. If Charles Shaw contacts you, tell him that you are aware of my efforts and totally support them. Thanks." I hope he reads his email soon.

"Where shall we begin?" I ask.

"Let's tour the perimeter together, but keep our observations private until we are done," Detective Nederfield is back in charge.

My cell phone buzzes that I have an email. *I have your back. Jung.* We got confirmation from Jung Kim that Mr. Shaw won't be a problem."

"Forward Ho!" Elias waves and starts whistling the tune from *Bridge over the River Kwai.* We all join, even the somewhat recalcitrant Deputy Silver.

Actually there is more of a Ward Bond feeling to our tour around both the perimeter and inside of the track facility. Elias leads about six vehicles from his department including a SWAT armored truck, an ambulance, three marked cars and a pick up truck loaded with orange cones which it periodically places where Sheila White points. We circle the wagons for about an hour and then repeat the tour on foot. Occasionally a cone is moved or an entry is made into one of the dozen open tablets carried by each of us.

"Thomas, are there schematics of the track?" The TSA head asks.

"I have all the plans in my office that have been filed with the Palm Beach County Building Department since the track was built," Sheriff Rosewood volunteers. "I have all the electric and plumbing diagrams as well. Now that Thomas has gotten us access, I have arranged for two of our county engineers to accompany any or all of you through every square inch of the place."

"Well done Elias." Chief Detective Nederfield is impressed.

"I took it from your playbook, Olivia. It's what you did for the Super Bowl," Sheriff Rosewood replies.

"I didn't know it was widely known," Olivia responds.

"The Sheriff of Miami-Dade County is a very close friend and he was impressed by you. He didn't know we were friends, so I played dumb and let him extol your brilliance."

"I think we should adjourn your mutual admiration society and have lunch," I suggest.

"Great idea," Agents Forbes and Driver shout from the back of our group.

"A van from the department is supposed to meet us with box lunches and drinks at the main entrance momentarily," Elias replies. "Then I think we should go back to my office and compare notes."

"Should I tell the SWAT guys and the other deputies to resume their regular duties? Detective Silver asks. I hope she isn't upset about Elias and me quipping back and forth in Seminole.

"Ask them if they want lunch. I want to see if there is anything we might have missed from their prospective. They are the ones who will be on the ground . . . together with your folks." Sheriff Rosewood directs his comment toward the assembled Feds.

"How many SWAT vehicles do you have available?" Sheila White asks.

"I've got four, but I can borrow some from other counties and the National Guard depending on how many you want to deploy," Elias answers.

"I can get some as well," FBI agent Forbes adds.

"Once we sweep the place and secure the entrances, we are in good shape. It's not going to be like the real race. Everyone will be inside the facility," I offer.

"I think we can do a lot with laser gridding to prevent unauthorized entry and exiting," Olivia observes.

"The less it looks like a fortress, the happier POTUS will be," Secret Service Agent Driver says.

"Let's have lunch. I'm starving," I suggest.

"Now that's a surprise." Olivia can be hurtful at times—a little.

CHAPTER THIRTEEN

I am amazed and pleased at how fast the time flies by. We approach Orlando a little before 5. Get it—time flies by. We actually accomplished a lot, however it falls upon my shoulders to update Tsarkis. I think that we have identified most, if not all, of the issues relating to physical and medical safety protocols and have divided up responsibilities amongst us. We are exploiting Deputy Silver's Intel background by placing her in charge of creating a virtual inventory of everything we will need for the event—and I mean everything from digital thermometers to explosive sniffing dogs to Humvees. Shelia White has assigned two TSA agents and Dan Driver has loaned a couple of Secret Service types to work with her—actually under her, which seems to have made Elias' sister less uptight. I imagine it is tough transitioning from being a Lieutenant Commander to a mere Sheriff's Deputy. At least I don't get any dirty looks anymore.

Everyone is suspiciously quiet when I raise the issue of procurement—like where do we get the money? Sure some things can be loaned from other agencies, but personnel costs money as does the per diem we have to pay the racers to travel to Palm Beach and back. I say *we* euphemistically because each and every tax paying American is paying a portion of this show and tell time.

"Who is best able to cost out the items Deputy Silver and her team lists?" I ask no one particular as we clear for landing at the Orlando Executive Airport.

"Thomas raises an excellent point." Olivia backs me up.

"All Secret Service agents will be paid from our budget," Dan Driver states.

"Same with FBI; including any equipment," Agent Forbes adds.

"TSA has been given a blank check by Homeland Security," Director White says.

"We can't ask the taxpayers of Palm Beach County to pay for the Sheriff's Department expenses," I state. "Also, Olivia and I are on loan from the Orange County Sheriff's office for this event. And who has jurisdiction over creating and enforcing a no fly zone?"

"May I suggest once you get everything we collectively need from Deputy Silver, we can each review the list and check off what we can supply. Everything else is the responsibility of the White House." Sheila's proposal makes sense. "Let's each go over today's walk through over the weekend, prepare memos to our respective seniors, but exchange them on the *QT* before submitting." I can fully understand how Sheila White became Director of TSA.

"I will send Tsarkis a quick email saying we met and I will get back to him late Monday. I can use our meeting with Jung Kim as an excuse." The tires of the Gulf Stream make that unique chirping sound upon touching ground.

"Olivia, Thomas, please let me know if there are any glitches concerning Palm Beach after you talk with Jung Kim. Call my cell anytime. I will set up a Zoom conference

Monday at noon and send everyone the link." Sheila Brown is efficient and if we ever fly anywhere, I'll feel that TSA is being well led.

The group disperses.

"What time do we have to leave tomorrow morning?" The gorgeous Chief Detective asks.

"It's less than a half hour, so we should leave around eight," I respond.

"Let's pick up some gazpacho and a baguette on the way home. We have a nice Chardonnay in the fridge. We have to pack. I will call the motor pool and tell them to pick up the Explorer at the Fairgrounds in the afternoon. Motor pool might be a tad put out if it's stolen or spray painted over night. We won't be back until Monday morning."

"A splendid plan, my dear. Simply splendid."

"Aren't you glad you didn't have to listen to Charles Shaw the whole day? Dropping Kim's name sent him scurrying into whatever hole he came from."

"Knowing people in high places has its advantages. I wonder if young Juan Carlos will be driving tomorrow. I know that he has competed in a couple of races in Argentina over the winter. He's a bit of a brat, but I think Uncle Jung will shape him up. I predict he will spend several years racing for Kim Tires on the junior circuit before he is even considered for the Trophy series. If he wins, it's a plus for marketing to the South American market. If not, it will be a learning experience," I comment.

"There is a certain irony that Don is driving the 31 with Kim sponsorship although their tires are only permitted in nonpoint's events. Do you think that will change?"

"NASCAR is going through a lot of changes, mostly positive. Competition amongst tire manufacturers is good for the sport in my opinion. It makes more money available to smaller teams and fosters product development," I answer. "The Kim family is patient and they have deep pockets, which insures staying power. The purchase of Gold Coast Raceway is an example of their commitment to the sport."

"Speaking of sponsors, I suspect that Don's family is also patient and has deep pockets as well. I wonder if pizza sales are up.

"Stop that! I'm getting hungry."

CHAPTER FOURTEEN

After sending Deputy Chief of Staff Tsarkis an email, check-ing my in box, mostly junk but not quite spam, Olivia and I enjoy the rest of the evening with our soup, bread dipped in olive oil and garlic and, of course, a bottle of wine. We decide to get up early for a run before heading over to the Fairgrounds. The day is finally catching up with us. We each dash through the shower, separately, set our alarms, turn off our cell phone ringers and crash—figuratively speaking.

Since I am usually going to a track each weekend, Saturdays and Sundays are seldom spent lying in bed and chilling. Unfortunately, Olivia has to punch the clock on Monday through Friday, so unless we are granted a day off for services rendered to our ogre boss, Sheriff Josh McCarthy, we are up and out by a little after 6.

Three quick miles, hot oatmeal with fresh berries I bought the other day, hot showers and we are out the door, with our over night bags. Our unmarked Sheriff's Explorer seems to encourage traffic to move aside with the result that we arrive at the Fairgrounds in twenty minutes, park in a VIP section, and head toward the concession stand for coffee. Usually the Junior circuit runs on the same track as the Trophy series and on the same weekend, albeit either Saturday afternoon or evening. Because of a charity exhibition event in Charlotte under the lights on Thursday, the Trophy practice and qualifying sessions are scheduled for Saturday, thus the split venue. Actually dividing the race groups is better for the younger drivers since none of the top tier drivers compete. It gives the up and coming kids a place to show case their talent against each other. It also means that Don Montgomery is in Atlanta while Kim Tires is drumming up business at the Fairgrounds in Orlando today.

Actually, Don's crew chief, Tim Sun, is one of Jung Kim's most trusted employees and although the 31 has to use tires from the company whose name shall not be uttered because it is a point's race, the Kim Tire logo is predominately displayed with the image of a slice of extra cheese and pepperoni pizza. It is understood that no one goes under hood except Tim Sun or Peter Corolatti, a member of Don's extended family, who pretends that he speaks no English although I have it from a good source that he graduated from Cal Tech. It is hilarious to see Tim and Peter *discussing* a mechanical issue. It sounds like the Tower of Babel without benefit of translators. Actually, it's more like some political big shot with a sign language interpreter. Lots of hand gestures. I guess their system works since the Camaro has no DNFs this season.

The day is picture perfect—mid 80s but no humidity.

"Let's get some java and then look for Jung Kim," I suggest.

"Two good ideas," Olivia responds.

I take a minute to realize that I actually made two suggestions. I guess I really need that cup of caffeine.

The line moves quickly. As we exit the concessions area, I hear, "Senorita Olivia and Thomas, I am so glad to see you."

Juan Carlos Cidado is in attendance. He rushes up to Chief Detective Nederfield, who is about six inches taller and kisses her on both cheeks. I am trying to stifle a laugh and not spill my coffee at the same time.

"Hola!" I exclaim. I am not sure how much Juan Carlos I can take. The last time I saw him he had just crashed into a wall at Daytona after a tire blew. He isn't a bad kid, just a bit full of himself and the silver spoon that goes with it.

Like the long lost brother or nephew, who he isn't, Juan Carlos greets us with the enthusiasm only someone from the land of the tango can. In about five minutes of non-stop blabbering, we now know everything that has happened since Daytona. The highs include his complete recovery from a broken arm, falling in love, breaking up, getting back into racing and coming to the United States to compete. He does not mention that although he is doing well, Don Montgomery is doing better in the same car with the same tires. Time will tell. At least, based on his performance in the last six races, he is learning to care for his machinery. No wreck is a good thing, especially if you are driving for Kim Tires.

"Detective Nederfield, Deputy Ballard, if you can spare a few minutes Mr. Kim can see you now," a young man wearing a matching shirt and cap featuring the new corporate logo announces.

"Adios Juan Carlos," Olivia shouts as we scurry after our messenger—and savior.

We are escorted to a gorgeous RV which seems to be fifty feet long; although I think the maximum length permitted is thirty-something. The young man demurely knocks and we are greeted by the managing director and CEO of Kim Tire, Jung Kim.

"Welcome my friends. Please come in." Turning to our escort, Kim says, "Thank you Mr. Park. Please make sure we are not disturbed." They exchange bows.

"It's been a busy year since we last saw you," Olivia observes. "You are making inroads, although more slowly than we would wish, into the world of competitive racing. The Junior circuit results are quite impressive."

"Thanks to your protégé, Mr. Montgomery, people are taking notice of us. We have had much pleasure from the nonpoint's races where we can almost double the tire life of the others. Sometimes I forget that the racing is the tail of the dog. Our sales of street tires has almost tripled, especially in South and Central America. "

"Congratulations. As I mentioned, we have come to seek your assistance in matters more befitting your alter ego," I say.

"Very eloquently stated Thomas. As we know, our lives weave a very intricate web. Tell me as much as you can," Jung Kim replies.

"We are authorized to tell you everything," Olivia inserts. "The premise is simple, but the devil is in the detail. Simply said, our President wants to stage a race for the members of the mini G-7 conference here in Florida . . . during the Formula 1 event."

"I am beginning to see many problems. Because our President has also been invited, several of my colleagues in Seoul have reached out to me. We are meeting on Tuesday and they will make me current. To have your insight will convince them that I have my finger in the soup. Is that the right expression?"

"Close enough," I reply. I spend the next fifteen minutes explaining the genesis of the entire operation to Jung Kim.

"I think that having the exhibition race at a different venue was a very cleaver solution to part of the problem. Your logistics are still a challenge, but you can compartmentalize the events."

"And the fact that you own the Gold Coast track makes it easier to keep the project reasonably quiet. I was already considering dumping Charles Shaw into the Everglades."

Jung starts to laugh. "He's a pompous ass. I have another way to silence him. Maybe not as rewarding, but reasonably effective. We are building a test track in Korea and his invaluable expertise is required on site . . . immediately." Jung chuckles again.

"Very effective . . . and very inscrutable." We all start to laugh.

Jung Kim picks up his cell phone and dials. He pushes a lot of buttons so I assume it is not a local call. Three minutes of speaking Korean to the person on the other end of the call, brings another smile to his face. "It is done. Mr. Shaw will be on a flight to Seoul. He has been told that his expertise is required on a very hush-hush project. That should be more than sufficient." Jung Kim dials another number followed by a knock on the door. "Enter." Our escort enters. "Mr. Park, I am placing you in charge of our testing facility in Palm Beach. An event is being planned and I want you to facilitate anything that either Miss Olivia or Mr. Thomas requests. It will mean working with local law enforcement as well as some people from Washington, D.C. The event will include our President as well as many heads of other countries. This is of paramount importance to everyone. Credentials will be prepared for you. Listen and learn. This is an opportunity to impress many important people."

"Pardon me for interrupting, but among the participants in the event are the Margaret and Hans Leiter and their group of very special people."

"Mr. Park, you will be introduced to seven extraordinary men and one unbelievable woman. Do not be deceived by their age or seemingly carefree attitude. They have been and still are the best in our business. Believe me. Hopefully there will be no need for you to observe their skills, but simply to meet them is an honor. If you can be ready in thirty minutes, I will have a driver take you to the Orlando Executive Airport. Our plane will take you to Palm Beach and someone from the track will pick you up. Tell no one why you are going except that you have been appointed interim manager of the testing facility. You will be there for at least sixty days. Lee Song will familiarize you with the track. He has been on site for almost a month and should be able to answer any questions you may have. If he cannot provide you with the information you need, call me directly and I will make sure the proper information is made available. On Wednesday, I will meet you in Palm Beach and hopefully Chief detective Nederfield and Deputy Ballard will join me." Jung Kim ever so slightly nods his head in our direction

I think we've gone from Miss Olivia and Mr. Thomas to titles to impress Mr. Park with our official status. Jung gets an A+ for efficiency, but given our previous interaction, I am not surprised. If the young man is surprised, intimidated or otherwise plussed, he doesn't give any indication. He simply nods and leaves.

Turning to us, Jung Kim says, "Chung Park may be young, but he has had a lifetime of experience. His father was Korean ambassador to the United Nations for twenty years. He knows that not knowing is only a problem if you don't ask."

That takes a minute to sink in, but it's true. Only a fool with an enlarged ego thinks he or she knows everything. I suspect that respect for the elderly in most Asian cultures is based on the theorem that age instills wisdom to be shared with each succeeding generation.

"Do you want me to make arrangements to have our team meet at the track on Wednesday?" Olivia asks.

"That would be most helpful. I have never worked with the representatives being sent from Seoul and having all the advance work in place will convince them of our preparedness."

"And your control of the situation," I add, which causes Jung Kim to smile, ever so slightly.

"It is always best to be prepared when dealing with bureaucrats, regardless of the country for which they work," Jung Kim replies. "Let me refresh your coffee before we stroll the paddock."

"We have already run into Juan Carlos," Olivia quips.

"He is learning that being my sister's step son means you have to work harder. There is a great expression in English: *tough love*. He is a good driver and because he is not so shy, he is becoming a good salesman. It will take time."

"And you are a patient teacher," Olivia adds.

On that note, we leave the luxury of Jung Kim's hotel on wheels and head over to the team's garage. A driver, who seems to be no older than 14 years old, is standing next to the car normally driven by Don Montgomery. To say he looks nervous is a gross understatement. He might make a good back story to my report about the event.

"Jung, please introduce us to your new driver," I ask.

"He seems so young," Olivia maternally says.

"He is. We were able to get a waiver for him to race in four events this year on the Junior circuit. Basically the races that do not coincide with the Trophy series. You would have enjoyed watching the old man, twenty-two-year-old Donald, giving advice to Chad. Telling him to be very respectful of the car, the track, and even the drivers. This is his first race for us at this level. He has won the kart series three years in a row and is doing well in the truck series."

"On Kim Tires, no doubt," I quip.

"No doubt. Come let us meet the young man."

We start toward the driver, who is trying to find a place to hide.

"Chad Collins, I would like you to meet some very good friends of mine, Chief Detective Olivia Nederfield and Thomas Ballard."

"The writer? I read everything you write." Chad Collins is very kind and I am flattered. He extends his hand to shake mine, but suddenly decides that fist bumping is both more socially acceptable nowadays and is also cool.

"It is my pleasure to meet you as well. Sadly I don't get to watch many truck races and it's been years since I have written about the kart kids, as I call you youngsters. My bad, because that's where the new generation of drivers start."

"Along with simulators, Thomas," Jung adds. "Don't forget that virtual racing is a very inexpensive way to recognize talent early."

"And I bet that Kim Enterprises manufactures some component for the simulators." Olivia is on her game.

"Quite right, Miss Olivia. We provide packages for the beginners and many after market add-ons. Even the experienced Trophy cup drivers recognize the need to keep in shape physically, but also to be as one with the track and the car spiritually; especially in the off season." Jung Kim bows ever so slightly in our direction. Turning toward young Chad, he continues. "How many live laps have you driven on this course?"

"Between practice and qualifying . . . about thirty," the nervous young man says.

"And how many virtually?"

"Over six hundred." Driver Collins is getting a little confidence in his voice.

"And how do your lap times compare?"

"Initially Sir, I was a bit cautious like Mr. Montgomery had instructed. But then I realized that I actually had a lot of laps under my belt and my real qualifying time was only about a half second slower than my fastest virtual time. Last night I drove about twenty laps on my computer and actually saw where I could improve."

"Where are you on the grid for the feature?" I ask.

"Outside fourth row, Mr. Ballard."

"Jung, later this month, I want to interview your drivers, who are amongst the youngest in the series, and ask them how accurately simulators reproduce actual race experiences and are they a tool or a toy?"

"I will do you one better, we are planning to build a facility at Gold Coast to house Kim simulators for tire testing and driver skill development. We want to answer the questions you ask so we will have a group of drivers with different skill levels drive the track both virtually and in real time. You are welcome . . . both of you . . . to join us as participants."

"Thomas, that would make a terrific article," Olivia suggests.

"I am somewhat old school and hold to the belief that there is nothing like seat time on a track in a moving race car with other competitors around you, especially when the *big one* occurs, but I am willing to be convinced."

"Mr. Ballard may I say something?" Chad asks. "Are you aware that many of the new virtual devices have monitors for pulse, heart rate, and reaction time? Mr. Kim's machines have the ability to program in other driver's characteristics including driving style and can create situations on a screen that is almost identical to the real thing except you don't get hurt and can repeat the scenario again and again to see if there is something you could have done as a driver."

"Chad, how old are you?" Olivia is talking maternalisticly again.

"I just turned 17 and will be entering Chicago Institute of Technology in the fall. This summer, in addition to driving on weekends, I am virtually attending a worldwide engineering program for kids interested in computer engineering. I'm sponsored by Kim Enterprises. Please excuse me; I have a check list that I need to complete before the race. According to Mr. Montgomery you have to trust your crew, but double check anyway." Young Collins turns and heads back to his *loaner*.

"He is simply a wonderful young man," I observe.

"And easy to teach . . . willing to learn. The contrast between Juan Carlos and Chad ultimately will make the difference between a world class engineer and driver and a tire salesman in Buenos Aires."

"We need to talk about signing him to a contract to drive for the Tessa/Kim Team," I propose in earnest, not in jest.

CHAPTER FIFTEEN

Racing in the lower circuits combines a good old family outing with an all out effort to impress potential sponsors. Money has become a very important part of racing at almost any level, except the men and women who opt for the vintage venues, which can be best explained by the fact that vintage drivers have already *been there, done that*. None, well almost none, have any aspirations of competing at higher levels. There is only one level of vintage racing and for as long as winning, trophies, and prize money are deemphasized, it will remain that way—we hope.

Both Tessa/Kim drivers show a great deal of promise. Surprisingly, Juan Carlos exercised caution passing slower cars which are trying to keep their line while not blocking faster cars. There were several occasions when last year's version of the young Argentinean would race up a car's tailpipe, but the new improved driver showed patience. Safer and easier on the brakes.

Chad Collins was solid. His passes were well thought out and made with precision and success. He finishes third, while Juan Carlos finishes sixth, but only about four seconds behind his teammate. Kim tires performed flawlessly.

Unfortunately, the races are only about 150 miles in length, negating some of the advantages of the Kim technology which allows the tire to wear better than the competition, reducing costly pit stops.

In as much as neither driver is old enough to drink alcohol, they are feted with iced green tea and honey, which is surprisingly thirst quenching. The cars are loaded onto the trailers and head south to Palm Beach, which has become headquarters for the Kim Racing Group, which includes our number 31. Both drivers return with the cars rather than become spectators at Atlanta. Jung Kim insists that drivers assist the crew in post race inspection and repair, if necessary. I agree that a driver is more invested in a car when he is responsible for its maintenance.

"We have two RVs for the trip to Atlanta. I have taken the liberty of putting you in our unit so we can chat during dinner about the event. We will stop by your car as we leave so you can pick up your things. The RV is set up for wireless internet should it become useful. I think you will like dinner. Li Chin is a fantastic cook."

I look at Olivia who looks at me at the same time. I am not sure how much information we can share with Jung if there is another party present.

"Miss Olivia, do not be concerned. Li Chin and I have been together for a long time. She was the Korean representative to the Interpol Council for almost ten years before she retired to become my personal assistant . . . and wife. She has full diplomatic credentials and is very intuitive about people. You will like her. She will be here after she makes sure the trailers are on the road and the passengers on the other RV are comfortable."

"Who are the other passengers, if I may ask?" I inquire of our host.

"They are distributors of our products. Several are going with us to Atlanta. It's a sales incentive to our biggest producers. We bring a different group every weekend. A very successful program. When I visit their offices there are always framed pictures of them with famous race car drivers." Jung Kim smiles and then rises in response the knock on the door.

"Good evening Chief Detective Nederfield and Deputy Ballard." A woman almost as tall as Olivia and every bit as stunning enters the RV. "May I call you Olivia and Thomas? I am Li Chin. I am looking forward to our road trip. Our driver is my brother Lu Chin and he is a member of the joint United States and Korean counter-terrorist task force."

From behind the divider between the living portion of the RV and the driving portion, a hand waives—for an instant— which is a good thing since we have gotten under way.

When ever I look at the floor of my truck, which is piled with newspapers, sticky notes and several pencils, but never fast food boxes, I comment to myself, *self, you need to get better organized*. After less than an hour of briefing, Jung has arranged transportation, lodging, food, sent his man to Palm Beach, set up a meeting, and brought along some heavy duty experts. And all I need to do is pick up the junk in my F-250.

"Would you like a cocktail, a beer, wine, or tea?" Li Chin asks.

"I would like a glass of white wine if you have it," Olivia answers.

"Me too," I add.

"Chardonnay or Pinot Grigio?" Our hostess replies.

"Chardonnay please," Olivia and I harmonize.

"Excellent choice," Jung Kim says. "The Pinot will go better with dinner. I hope you don't mind spicy food."

"Brother, some tea and honey?" Li Chin asks. Again the hand appears from behind the divider with a *thumbs-up*.

"Jung? The usual?"

"Thank you, my dear."

After we get our wine and Lu Chin his tea, Li Chin hands her husband a small glass with amber liquid and one ice cube. She pours herself a glass of wine. "Cheers!" She raises her glass and we follow.

"Before you ask, I was on assignment in England several years ago and was enthralled with Scotland, especially the fishing and the Scotch. I decided what I liked and had the distiller blend me my own special Scotch. I order 20 cases each year. I limit myself to a single two ounce drink each evening. It is a simple vice. If you are a Scotch drinker, I would be pleased to offer you some."

"I seldom drink hard liquor although a well-aged Bourbon or Scotch has been known to pass my lips. I will take a rain check until tomorrow after the race."

Jung Kim lifts his glass and takes a sip. "Our journey takes between nine and ten hours. We will travel non-stop since Lu Chin is a very experienced chauffeur." Again the hand appears and waves. "Although I hate to mix business with pleasure, I would appreciate it, Thomas, if you would go over everything from the beginning. Please do not feel like you are repeating yourself, but getting all the data at one time may help us focus our energies."

"Olivia, jump in if I miss anything," I add.

For the next 40 minutes, while the RV navigates around Saturday evening traffic—mostly lost tourists—I go over the entire genesis of the event and what we have put in place as far as our team and its resources are concerned.

"That was very thorough. Thank you, Thomas." Jung Kim turns to Li Chin, "Any questions?"

"Yes, I have a question," the voice behind the screen asks. "Is there any Intel that suggests that any kind of effort to disrupt either event is pending?"

"None of which we are aware." I think I am shouting because I am not sure how good the acoustics are in the front. Only a handful of people know about the Palm Beach event. We are trying to keep all the planning as quiet as possible."

"When more than one person knows a secret, there is always a risk," Jung Kim opines.

"I suggest that it is time for dinner. We can all, how do you say, *sleep on it* and revisit everything in the morning," Li Chin says.

"Can I help with anything?" Olivia asks.

"If I can move the two men from their recliners, I can set up the dining area. All the food is already prepared and ready to serve."

We take our cue and shift to the front of the RV. With the push of a button, the living room becomes a dining room.

"Are you comfortable with chop sticks?" Li Chin asks.

"I may need a spoon," Lu Chin shouts and everyone starts to laugh.

"And a bib," his sister replies.

Neither Olivia nor I know a lot about Korean cuisine except that we like it.

"Traditional Korean food consists of five main colors," Li explains. "Green, red, yellow, white, and black, each signifying a direction, a natural element and a health benefit."

"Li has prepared two main dishes, so you can try different flavors, textures, and smells,' Jung Kim explains. "Bibimbap is a mixture of rice, vegetables, beef, what we call gochujang or hot chili paste and a fried egg. It's our comfort food."

"There is nothing in Western foods quite like Haemul Pajeon, which is a rice and egg pancake, very crunchy, filled with seafood. I hope you enjoy." Our hostess begins to serve us dinner in bowls which makes it a lot easier to eat. Unbelievably delicious.

"It is now almost ten, and we should all retire. Olivia and Thomas, your room is on the left. The bathroom is immediately across. We are in the back. I expect that we will be at the track around 6:30 which will give us plenty of time to freshen up.

CHAPTER SIXTEEN

I could get accustomed to traveling this way rather than towing my trusty vintage Airstream—well sometimes. Nelly Belle, that's Olivia's name for our home away from home, is great for four day events provided there is a shower close by. The polished aluminum sided classic always brings out admirers. However, Jung's hotel on wheels is an entirely different world, especially since someone else is driving. We arrive at the designated paddock at 6:30 as promised. The track surface is rough and needs work, but the amenities are up to date, especially the showers. Since most teams travel in RVs, the demand on the more public facilities is reduced, leaving me plenty of hot water. Having become a bit of a track rat herself, Olivia follows my lead and joins me. Actually, each shower is in its own little room, so fraternizing is discouraged. I think Li Chin and Jung Kim appreciate a bit of private time.

The dawn brings action to the Trophy series participants. The smell of fresh coffee permeates the air. It's a Starbucks moment. We are dressed for the day: jeans, comfortable walking shoes and matching Tessa/Kim shirts. As overseer of the team, as distinguished from owner, which is a story onto itself, our shirts are the white button down Oxford style, sleeves rolled up, embroidered with the team logo, a slice of Tessa pizza partially inside the center of a Kim tire. We intentionally do not have our names or team position on our shirts. As a journalist, I don't want people to try out their latest theories on me and as a team major domo, I don't want to deal with salespersons. As a 6'2" beautiful, blonde cop, Olivia doesn't want to be on a first name basis with anyone she doesn't already know or may not want to know.

The crew wears Polo type shirts, also embroidered with the pizza tire. None of their shirts have their name either, but for altogether different reasons. I learned from a friend and sometimes colleague, who outfits the Bentley Seven plus one that clean shirts are the sign of a well run team and that he always has an ample supply of spares. Crew members are encouraged to swap out his or her dirty shirt with a clean one of the same size. A very communal and inclusive policy.

The door of the RV opens and since there were only five of us, I assume it is Lu Chin, all 6'4" 250 pound linebacker of him. "Good morning. We did not get to meet yesterday. I am Lu Chin, your wheel man, bodyguard, brother-in-law of the boss, and a few other things."

"So we understand. If you have any questions about last evening's briefing let us know."

"Miss Olivia, Mister Thomas, at this point in time, I am going to take a hot shower, put in my ear plugs, and try to get about eight hours of sleep. I have to repeat the trip tonight. I have never visited the facility in Palm Beach, so I am not able to comment about strategic planning, but after Wednesday, I will feel free to share my thoughts with you." Lu bows and ambles away.

We continue toward the RV. The door opens again and Li Chin emerges holding two steaming mugs. "Good morning. I noticed you met my brother. I hope he wasn't too grumpy. He gets that way when he doesn't get his beauty rest. It's a perfect day for a race. Hot temperatures on a rough track. Someday Kim tires will win their first Trophy race on a day like today." She's all team.

Li Chin is also wearing the executive, nameless team shirt, tucked in and proper. Both Olivia and I have our shirt tails hanging out. Heck, it's Florida, but flip flops are definitely a *no no* at the track.

"Coffee smells fantastic," Olivia mutters as she drinks.

"The beans are Columbian. One of Jung's distributors has a family coffee plantation and sends us a pound a week of whatever blend they think we will like. I am not sure that we have ever gotten the same blend twice, but we are hooked. Tea is fine at dinner, but freshly ground beans brewed with purified water starts each morning perfectly."

"This is the best coffee I have ever tasted. I can't imagine ruining it with cream or sugar," I add.

"Li Chin, I don't want to seem rude, but how long have you and Jung been together?" Olivia asks.

"Our families have been close for several generations. Jung and I grew up together. We have been married for almost twenty years. He is much older than I am."

"I heard that!" Jung says exiting the RV holding two mugs. After handing one steaming mug to Li, he continues. "I am exactly nine days older than my dear bride."

"Only nine? It seems like nine hundred." They both start to laugh.

We join them in mirth until a voice shouts, "I am glad to find you all together." It's Tim Sun, the crew chief followed closely by Don Montgomery. "There is a serious problem here at the track."

"Please explain." Tim Sun is a little out of breath so Don takes over. "The track is literally shredding tires. Not just ours, but everyone's. Instead of having a fuel/tire window of 48-54 laps, I think that under race conditions, the tires will start coming apart around 25 laps, maybe earlier. I envision a lot of fender benders . . . or worse."

"I must think about this in consultation with Thomas." Jung sounds circumspect. "Please prepare the car for the race as usual." Both Tim and Don fast walk back toward the garages.

"We have some fresh fruit and pastries in the kitchen. Let us refresh our coffee and talk this through." Li Chin corals us into the RV.

"We must talk openly but only with each other until we have developed a strategy," Jung Kim says.

"Don't worry about me, I'm sleeping." The voice of Lu Chin booms from behind the curtain. We all begin to laugh again.

"There are two ways to play this out and I am not thrilled with either," I suggest. "Both are dangerous, but in entirely different ways."

We spend the next half hour sipping coffee, nibbling pastry and considering how to deal with the news Don related. After a lot of *what if's*, we agreed on a plan.

"What time do the pre race activities begin?" Olivia asks.

Li taps a few keys on her laptop. "About 11:30, a little less than two hours from now. I think we should ask Tim and Don to join us. Also Peter Corolatti. What we decide will impact all of us."

I text Don and Jung texts Tim. Within a few minutes, the trio arrives. "Coffee?" Our hostess asks.

"Yes, please," the young driver replies.

"Si, grazie," Peter adds.

Tim simply shakes his head from side to side.

"We would like to share our thoughts with you," Jung begins. "We either all agree or we simply don't implement the plan. OK?"

Everyone nods.

"If anyone has any questions, please wait until we have finished. We have given this a great deal of thought and have tried to anticipate both short-term and long-term responses to our proposal." I am a little nervous but resolved.

After a ten minute briefing, the RV was silent.

"Bravo!" Peter Corolatti shouts.

Tim Sun simply nods.

"It certainly could be a game changer. And I feel comfortable with your analysis. It gives us a clear direction, but also a fall back position. Let it begin here." Don's enthusiastic reception makes me feel a lot better.

"Peter, can you handle the pit?" I ask.

"Si!"

"And Tim, you need to make sure the on-track logistics are perfect." I continue.

"I understand and am willing to accept the responsibility. Thank you for your confidence in me." Tim bows his head first toward Jung Kim and then toward Li Chin.

"I guess my nap is over," Lu Chin bellows as he emerges from behind the screen wearing a Tessa/Kim pit crew fire suit, holding his gloves and helmet. "We may need to change a lot of tires."

"Thank you." Jung Kim bows his head.

"Let's go team!" Olivia is on her feet. "Everyone out!"

CHAPTER SEVENTEEN

The pre-race pageantry is a bit much. This car race not the Rose Bowl Parade. After march-byes, fly-overs, acknowledgements by management, an invocation, and the singing of our National Anthem by the tenth runner up at some talent show, the drivers finally get into their cars. The race is scheduled for 250 laps with the first two stages being 65 laps each, outside the normal pit cycle for tires and gas. But this is not going to be a normal race. After five pace laps the green flag is waved. The lap times are quite good although the track temperature is nearing one hundred twenty degrees. As predicted by our young, but astute driver, tires start to shred by lap 22. The right front tire of the 91 literally disintegrates along the front straightaway sending the disabled car into the wall under the start/finish line. That got a lot of people to pay attention. The driver was able to keep the Toyota along the wall and not cross the track onto the infield grass. The yellow flag slowed the cars as the wreck was removed. Pit lane opened and most the lead cars quickly entered for gas and new tires. Don stayed out. Jung Kim left our paddock and quickly walked along the pit wall where all the recently changed tires were piled. After looking at a couple of tires, he quickly returned to our pit box and nodded at Tim Sun, who told the number 31 to come in for tires and gas. Pit lane was a bit of a chaos. Crews were staring in disbelief at the rubber carcasses, since they could hardly be called tires. Don slid to a stop and the Tessa/Kim crew quickly changed all four tires and topped up the gas tank. 13.4 seconds. Good enough to move up two positions and move into eighth.

After the race resumes, I say, "Now the fun begins."

As the cars approach the final four laps before the end of the first stage, several cars suffer tire failures. The pace slows a bit although the yellow remains furled. Our driver moves up a couple of positions, but not too many. With two laps to go, Tim tells Don to *hot foot it*. The 31 deftly passes four cars and then simply pushes the Camaro around the high line, taking the green and white checker, while accumulating valuable points. The pits open and everyone comes in. Tires are changed all around, except on Don's car. Lu Chin walks around the car, examining each tire by placing a temperature gauge on the surface. The fuel cell is again filled and Don Montgomery exits. 7.6 seconds.

As the track temperature rises, failures are more frequent. By the end of the second stage, which is also won by our car, although only by three car lengths, most teams have used six sets of tires, and there are still 120 laps to go.

Pit lane opens and the competitors enter to put on their last set of tires. The 31 changes right side only. 9.9 seconds. Several drivers try to draft past Don on the restart. Tim instructs him to let them, but to keep pressure on the lead cars. *Make them go faster*. Don picks off the leaders one at a time. Precisely, but not conspicuously.

The *big one* happens on lap 158. Two cars entering turn one next to each other, almost simultaneously experience tire failure. Their cars start to spin uncontrollably. The resulting carnage is huge. At least ten cars are totally trashed and another seven are heavily damaged and unlikely to be able to compete. The race is red flagged. There is debris everywhere. Our car stops along the wall on turn three, the only portion of the track that is in the shade. I have to smile at Don's presence of mind. Once the wreckage is removed the remaining cars slowly drive to pits and line up in their former running position. The Tessa/Kim Camaro is first.

Tim Sun makes a slicing gesture across his throat. Then the public address system announces that the race has been cancelled. There is a tire shortage and safety is paramount.

"There is a tire shortage because there was a shortage of good tires," I suggest.

The Tessa/Kim team quickly surrounds the 31 and begins to push it to the winner's circle. If more than half the scheduled laps are completed, the car leading at the instant of the red flag is the winner—Donald Montgomery. We know that the s**t is about to hit the fan. The post race inspection will tell it all.

"Thomas, as team owner, please join me," Jung Kim says. He marches off toward the control tower. We pick up a couple of Georgia State Troopers on our journey, one of whom I met on another matter. The door at the base of the tower suddenly opens and two rather red faced race executives confront us.

"I will see that you two are banned from racing for life," the first suit says.

"Is that going to be before or after I write several pieces for every automotive outlet in the world?" I'm pissed. I do not like to be threatened.

"Deputy Ballard, calm down. I'm sure Mr. Potter's comment was made in jest," My trooper colleague says.

"Deputy Ballard? I thought you are a writer," Suit number two says. I know I've seen his face, but I can't place him.

"Gentlemen, my name is Jung Kim and I am the executive director of Kim Tires and we have proved to you today that we make a product able to withstand the harshest track conditions without failure. It would not be good for the sport if the failure rate of tires is disclosed. You can talk about innovation in the racing world and that in an effort to explore all technologies; you gave permission to Kim Tire to put its rubber on the 31 in an effort to evaluate its performance. There may be a little fallout, but it can be contained. This is a new era and you are expanding the concept of inclusion to products. It will make the sport more contemporary and make everything more competitive giving rise to innovation."

"Mr. Potter, we have never met, but as a person whose life has been spent as a journalist, I know enough to know that if you are given lemons, make lemonade. You are being given a choice between a public relations nightmare and a five star review. And I am a Sheriff's deputy in Florida and have worked with Georgia law enforcement on a rather touchy matter."

"Which got us a five star review and not a black eye because of Deputy Ballard and his team." I am glad our escort remembered me.

"We had better get over to the Winner's Circle and present your young driver with his trophy," Suit number two says.

"And I thought this was going to be a relaxing Sunday at the track," I whisper to Jung.

"But it has been most productive. Most productive. Let's return to the ladies who are probably chaperoning Donald and keeping those young girls in the short, tight shorts away from him."

I can just imagine Olivia and Li flanking our protégé surrounded by confetti and champagne. Pizza and beer come later.

CHAPTER EIGHTEEN

The next three and a half weeks are chock-a-block full of preparations, attendance at both meetings and races—I do have a
day job—and simply trying to keep one's head above water.
Thanks to the Orange County Mayor, the Commissioners,
the Mayor of Orlando, and the big wigs at both Universal
and Disney, everything falls into place. Executive orders are
entered and immediately ratified banning firearms. Local,
state, and federal health agencies create protocols. The *attrac-
tions* will give free admission to all race participants. The airport will provide additional ground service to the track. The
track developers had the foresight to build a SunRail station
at Citrus Grove so that spectators can easily access the track
for both automotive and musical events. I even finished the
press credential process without too many complaints.

The track owners, with the help of the local building
inspector, install a six hundred person temporary skybox
along the back straightaway with real toilets, carpeting, A/C,
and three bars. All VIPs; whether foreign dignitary, corporate
giant, or county commissioner, will sit in the new sky box if
they don't have season tickets to the luxury suites across the
track. Period.

Palm Beach is an entirely different story. We are getting tons of cooperation from local political folks. Even the gang from D.C. is moving Heaven and Earth to find the resources to ensure a safe event. Needless to say, Jung Kim and his team are invaluable. Our transportation problems are minimal since we only expect less than one thousand people including all the competitors and their crews. So what can be the trouble one might ask? Each of the attendees of the G-7 (including the Koreans) has their own take on how the event should be choreographed: photo ops, meet and greet, tours of the track, entertainment (as if the racing isn't enough), and food. Oh, I forgot that everyone has an opinion of how security should be handled.

I know I don't get paid enough (which is nothing) for all this, but Sheriff Rosewood, Chief Detective Nederfield, TSA chief White, and the dozens of other dedicated law enforcement personnel also don't need to take s**t from some twenty something advance man or woman. Our colleagues are extremely adept at getting folks to reach a consensus, which is usually to let the people with the most knowledge of the facility protect it. That's us.

Even though the conference is supposed to be limited to the heads of the most powerful economies in the world, the meeting attracts a lot of wannabees from other nations, who naturally want to be included. Many of these *other leaders* are not good at taking *no* for an answer. Our team reached the boiling point about ten days before the event when a certain spoiled rich kid from a certain oil rich desert Middle Eastern country demanded that he and his entourage be included. Without the advice and consent of my colleagues, except Jung, whose counsel is always well thought out, I call

Assistant Deputy Chief of Staff Tsarkis. I don't email him. I don't text him, I call him.

"Nicholas, Thomas Ballard here. You have a problem. Not we have a problem, but you have a problem. Our entire team is quitting. Since you do not have any jurisdiction over the majority of us, we can simply pack up and leave. Good luck."

"I don't understand. What's wrong?" He sputters.

"G-7 means seven heads of state, not eight or eleven or twenty. No one except the members of the mini-conference will be permitted on the premises. Period. The Gold Coast Raceway will become suddenly unavailable for the event. Too bad. The State Department can handle the fallout."

A much calmer Nicholas Tsarkis says, "I get it. My people on the ground are feeling the same way."

"So why did you wait until I called you?"

"Sometimes problems go away by themselves," Nichols responds.

"The only way this problem is going to disappear is if certain people, who shall for the time being remain anonymous, are immediately placed on a plane or planes and sent packing. Your call. Remember, we have two back to back events hundreds of miles apart to run and this one is far less important that the Formula One event at Citrus Groves. You all have been extended every possible courtesy to pull this off. Remember this entire show is to save your butt. I am letting everyone have the balance of the day off. You've got until 8 o'clock tomorrow morning." I hang up. I feel a lot better. Although I cannot hold a tune, I start to whistle on my way to our makeshift headquarters at the garages.

"You sound chipper," Sheriff Rosewood observes.

"Yup," I answer.

"Man of few words."

"Yup."

"Are you going to keep me in suspense?"

"Nope." I pause just long enough to begin pissing off Elias. Just a bit. "We are all taking the rest of the day off compliments of the White House. Spread the word."

"Should I ask why?"

"Nope."

"That works." He walks off calling to everyone he sees.

I haven't seen Olivia or Sheila in some time. Dollars to donuts they are not on Worth Avenue, although I suspect they might like to be. Those two are so conscientious it gives me a headache, but I'm glad they are on our team. I speed dial.

"Hey gorgeous, how would like the rest of the day off? We can stroll the avenue and then have an early dinner, wherever, compliments of the White House deputy chief of staff."

"Wow! How did you finagle that?"

"We're entitled. The suits sit around in luxury while we work in the sweltering Florida heat and humidity." I think we are entitled.

"Can Sheila come along?"

I had anticipated the question. The two have become friends and other than Elias' sister, the less than effervescent, Deputy Rachael Silver, there aren't any other women in our group.

"Absolutely. The day off invitation extends to the entire team and Sheriff Rosewood is spreading the word. Maybe I will ask Li Chin and Jung Kim. But no shop talk."

Olivia puts her hand on her cell phone. I hear garbled talking. "Sheila is thrilled. We'll meet you at the start/finish line in fifteen minutes. We just need to freshen up."

"In fifteen minutes?"

"With Worth Avenue as the bait, we could probably be ready in ten minutes."

I knew they had shopping on the brain. I dial Jung's cell and invite them to join us. He quickly accepts, but before he hangs up Li comes on the phone.

"I will have Mr. Park get us a car and driver. Parking on Worth Avenue can be difficult. Jung says fifteen minutes at start/finish. Thank you for including us, Thomas. Fortunately I have been somewhat removed from your activities, but setting up the computer system for our testing program has been time consuming, but rewarding."

Needless to say, the ladies go off shopping, or at least window shopping, since being a civil servant on one of the nation's most expensive streets limits one's ability to purchase. As it turns out, Jung Kim and I both share an interest in old books and we easily pass the time away browsing several very awesome shops. Jung was tempted by a first edition, second printing of *A Tale of Two Cities*, but the condition, not the price, deters him. How nice to be able to afford anything, but also how refreshing it is to be with someone who is willing to wait for what he wants rather than being a compulsive buyer. I sense the Kim family is not compulsive about anything.

As planned we meet Olivia, Sheila, and Li at *The Seafood Shack*, which is not exactly a shack, but a very chic restaurant, serving fantastic fish. Thank you 1600 Pennsylvania Avenue. We are shown today's acquisitions, which surprise me at the quantity and cost. I guess we will be eating beans and franks for a while at home.

"You are never going to believe what happened." Olivia's opening line is a bit perplexing.

I take the bait. "No I'm not going to believe what happened. What happened?"

"We walked into this over the top boutique. Every designer in the world has some line in the store. A man rushes over to us and says *you three are right on time*."

"That is very believable," Jung Kim replies.

"No! No! You don't understand," Sheila White exclaims. She's right, we don't understand.

"The man who approached us is the owner of the boutique and he was planning a photo shoot when two 6 foot tall women; one blonde and the other Asian, and their red headed, green eyed pale skinned, friend walk in. He becomes very agitated and asks us if we are his models. Before we are able to say a word, he has his assistant, Peter his name tag said, literally push us into a large dressing room with racks of gorgeous clothes," Li adds.

"Well, what's a lady to do? We try on clothes and are photographed. An hour later, the owner starts clapping and says that we are the best models he has ever worked with. No chit chat—just business. Just then, three women walk in, actually sashay in, and announce that they are sorry they are late but they couldn't find a parking place. The owner looks perplexed, but cool and tells the three that he was on a schedule and hired other models, dismissing the threesome with a wave of his hand."

"What agency sent you? I am thrilled."

"*We are just three ladies walking down the Avenue admiring the all the gorgeous clothes, I said.*" Olivia obviously is in her element.

"But you three were so exquisite and so professional," the store owner stuttered. "And the photos are perfect. May I use them?" He hesitated. "I will gladly pay you. I need your names for the photo credits. Can you come back for the fall line?"

"I have a suggestion, just issue each of us a house charge and we will use it to purchase some items," Li suggests.

"Excellent. Peter, each of these lovely ladies has a six hundred dollar line of credit. Is that satisfactory?" The store manager asks.

"I tell him that it is a perfect resolution," Olivia inserts. "We give him our names, more or less. So here we are after having a wonderful afternoon spending someone else's money."

"Maybe I should have bought that first edition." Both Jung and I start to laugh.

"Well done ladies. If ever I need someone to forage for me, I'll look you up. You know that by giving him alias names, you have given up promising careers." I am trying to stifle another laugh. This kind of stuff only happens in movies—or mystery novels.

Dinner is scrumptious—so is the food. The conversation is as varied as the participants. I beckon the waiter and ask for the check.

"The treat is mine," Jung says. "I haven't had such a pleasant day in a long time."

"Actually, it's a treat of the President of the United States. I told his deputy chief of staff that unless he got rid of a certain obnoxious Middle Eastern brat, we were cancelling the event. I told him we were taking the day off. I didn't mention dinner, but it is going on my expense account."

We rise to leave when suddenly a voice, attached to a frantically running man waving his arms who says, "Thank goodness I have found you." Jung and I look at each other. "Pardon me, I am Joseph Scarletti and I own the store where these beautiful women posed for a photo shoot this afternoon. I forgot to get your contact information so I can recommend you to my many friends and also have you return in a few months."

The ladies look at each other and nod. Each one removes a business card from their wallets and hands them to Mr. Scarletti. He looks at the cards, then at the three and then at the cards again.

"You play a joke on Scarletti?" he says.

Each woman then retrieves an official identification badge from their pocket books. This time Scarletti turns as white as a sheet.

"It is okay. We really enjoyed the afternoon and your store is fantastic. Please use our images. They belong to you. We were compensated. Needless to say, it is highly unlikely that we will be able to pose for either you or your friends in the future," Olivia explains. She extends her hand to shake, but he lightly kisses her finger tips.

"Thank you. All of you." He slowly backs away, turns and walks down Worth Avenue.

A dropped pin would make more noise.

CHAPTER NINETEEN

Upon our return to Chez Kim, Li offers us all a cup of tea and honey.

"It is still early, so I think we should review our schedules," Jung Kim suggests.

"We haven't heard from Tsarkis yet and I meant what I said. For over six weeks we have been working night and day and I am quite fed up with the Beltway folks dictating to us. The Formula One race has been in planning for years and the G-7 event for weeks. I don't suffer fools well." I try not to raise my voice.

"Thomas, I heard from the Deputy Chief of Staff about two hours ago by text. I think he is afraid of you. I didn't want to interrupt our most pleasant dinner. He said that the problem has been neutralized."

"I didn't mean to get the kid killed, just out of my hair."

"I assure you the Prince is resting well on his family's jet heading home. American movies tend to attribute words to rather limited meanings. Suffice it to say we have a full day tomorrow. Sheriff Rosewood has been made aware that his team is to assemble for . . . roll call at 0800. This weekend Li and I are flying to Kentucky for the Blue Grass 400. I will be your surrogate since I suspect that your collective dance card is rather full." Jung chuckles. "It is a nonpoint's event and I have been given permission to provide tires to two other teams, the number 89 Mustang and the 44 Toyota. Neither car is a front runner so management thought it was a safe bet neither would be in contention."

"You may be giving them a minute or more tire changing advantage over the course of the race," I insert.

"I certainly hope that and better gas mileage and better overall performance."

"This will be Don's first long distance race on Kim tires," Olivia says. "I wish we could go."

"Jung, why don't you send back the plane to Orlando Saturday late afternoon for Olivia and Thomas? We can all fly back after the race," Li Chen proposes. "You will have the entire next week to attend to the last minute details."

"Since we are, how do you say, brainstorming, why don't we open the track on Saturday instead of early Monday so that the cars can set up in relative calm? Offer the vintage folks a little track time, even a warm up race. Any Formula One driver who wants to familiarize himself or herself with the track can drive some laps in one of the Kim test cars. All informal and all low key," Jung Kim inserts.

"Herself?" Li Chin asks.

"Ferrari now has a woman driver on their team. She came out of kart racing and of course, simulators," I answer.

"My, we certainly have come a long ways." Olivia and Li fist bump.

"Let us celebrate with a glass of Korean rice wine, Cheongju. It is very strong and will give you a very restful sleep," Li Chin offers.

"Like our desert prince?" I hope I don't sound too sarcastic.

"His cocktail probably didn't taste as good." Jung Kim smiles.

"I want to extend the invitation to arrive early to Sir Bertram and Marshall Leventhal, especially the latter, since most of the teams will be trailering in, they may as well come directly to Gold Coast. They're more a Worth Avenue crowd than Mickey and Mini anyway."

"Li and I volunteer to show the vintage group all the best places to shop." The ladies bump fists again.

"We are going to spend tomorrow going over perimeter security with Elias and Sheila. The medical protocols are going to be the same at both tracks. I will need a list of media members for the Monday event no later than tomorrow afternoon. I assume they will have been vetted so all they will need is the press kit. That reminds me, I have to proof read the media package for the F-1 event and have it sent out by Friday." I am glad that we have ten days before the first participant appears.

"Jung has loaned me a couple of his tech guys to go over communication and surveillance both here and in Orlando. It will be a huge help. Some of the suits from the FBI resisted at first, but Agent Forbes carries a lot of juice in high places. I suspect his title is understated."

"When do you intend to return to Citrus Grove?" Li Chin asks.

"If you don't mind us imposing for another two nights, we will leave first thing Thursday and work through Saturday afternoon. I want to spend the following Monday, Tuesday and Wednesday in Orlando and then come back here. If your invitation is accepted, racers and their rigs should be arriving on Saturday. I am going to send out all the protocols for the competitors, regardless of venue, before we leave for Kentucky. Once we hear back from Sir Bertram and Marshall, we can plan track time for the weekend. I am being a bit disingenuous because what I really want is to give all our screening procedures a dry run with a small number of teams arriving over a couple of days. If there's a glitch, it can be fixed in advance both here and at Citrus Grove."

"Hardly disingenuous, Thomas. It is a very good solution. Making sure everything works under live conditions is essential. When we were talking about simulators as tools to teach racing techniques, we said that most conditions can be projected, analyzed and synthesized into real time. What cannot be simulated is how people will react. We can try to condition responses, but we are limited to those circumstances we anticipate. Next weekend, in addition to the race teams, I suggest we create controlled chaos. Not a lot, but just enough to make sure the people on the ground are aware that there are unknowns to be considered. Li Chin has been working on a program to insert both electronic and human unknowns into the equation throughout the weekend. We don't want surprises on Monday or the rest of the week in Orlando."

"You are absolutely spot on," Olivia says. "We try to replicate real life when we train, but the *x-factor* is always out there. I love the idea."

I simply put my hands together and bow.

"A toast!" Li Chin pours an almost clear liquid into four wine glasses.

"Where's mine?" Lu Chin's voice booms from the driver's compartment.

"We should always look behind the curtain. A spy could be lurking." Jung Kim lifts his glass.

CHAPTER TWENTY

We are both totally wiped out. Between macro managing her regular case load, micro managing the preparation of Palm Beach, and just plain managing the F-1 event, Olivia has not been home before ten o'clock any evening this week. I have been keeping the home fires bright and working the phones, texts, and emails. Marshall Leventhal and his hearty band of vintage formula drivers think that a couple of extra days at Gold Coast playing with their toys is a great idea. I will tell him that the track will open at 8 am on Saturday and we will schedule three open practice half-hour sessions. On Sunday, there will be a short warm-up session and two twenty lap races. Because we have a limited number of experienced corner workers, anyone acting out will be black flagged for the balance of both events. Elias has made arrangements for on track medical and towing services. The health and security protocols will be in place when the first competitor arrives. Li's special effects remain the *x-factor*.

The Formula One group is a little less flexible. They are more interested in getting set up at Citrus Grove, than extra time at Gold Coast. The former means money and the latter is simply for show as far as the teams are concerned. But at least fifteen cars have committed to Monday. The Ferrari team and the Mercedes team, each with young drivers, will be arriving Saturday for orientation and so-called seat time in the high tech Kim tricked out cars. Each of these test cars is fitted with more data gathering gear than a NASA space capsule. Every component in the car has a measuring device. Every driver is monitored for cardiac, pulmonary, muscle, and nerve responses. The cars are better equipped than most hospitals. When these events are over, I want to go to a driver's school at Kim racing headquarters. Simulators are the wave of the future, I guess, but these cars are super cool.

By noon on Saturday, we are counting the minutes before boarding the Kim corporate jet for the Blue Grass 400. Don's qualifying has placed him in the fifth row. The 44 and 89 have both gridded on the ninth row, which is their highest ever. In addition to Kim tires the two independents have had a little of Peter Corolatti's expert assistance in suspension set up and brake balance. The weather forecast is as expected: warm—like real hot—but dry. Keeping the car cool is important, but keeping the driver cool is equally, if not more, important. Kim Enterprises uses the standard driver A/C unit but has added a misting component to keep the driver hydrated. The 44 and the 89 also received the mystifying mister. What a waste of alliteration.

As the sleek sliver and blue jet taxies up to the Orlando Executive Airport terminal, we decide that hanging around with Jung and Li could be habit forming. Two hours later we pass through the track gate. Our driver pulls up to a very nice but pedestrian RV. Out host and hostess greet us with genuine warmth.

"I am sorry for our downsized accommodations, but Lu is in meetings with the security people for the G-7 and a sixteen hour drive is not what I do," Jung Kim says. I'd forgotten about Lu's day job with the joint counter terrorism task force. "Two hours by jet and a rental RV. Much more restful."

It works for me.

"Thank you for inviting us. We both needed to get out of Florida for a day," Olivia says.

"Correct me if I am incorrect but you are the team owner Thomas and Olivia is the chief . . . chaperone." Li bows slightly and then burst into a totally undignified but extremely warm laugh.

"By executive order, signed by me, there will be no discussion of either the exhibition race or the F-1 event!" I decree.

Everyone bows

"Before you ask, the jet is also a rental. Well, actually a time-share. My brother came up with the idea of starting an international rent-a-jet program. Having a single corporate plane for a company with personnel all over the globe makes no economic sense. Very expensive. He bought a fleet of fifteen Gulf Stars, has them based world wide and using a subscription model, has over a hundred companies each paying an annual fee as well as a usage fee. The entity is self-sufficient and may even make a profit. We have ordered another dozen planes, since we have a waiting list of customers."

"Is there anything Kim Enterprises doesn't do?" I hope my question doesn't sound snotty.

"There are many things," Li Chin starts, "but that is mostly because there are not enough hours in the day. That is the reason for the planes and for the myriad of electronic devices and applications developed by us."

"Please put your bags in the RV and wash up. There is a reception for drivers and owners. I would like you to meet Lincoln Taylor, the driver of the 44 and Harriet Ubana, driver of the 89. They are not only appreciative of the help we have been able to give them, but are both part of the new inclusion program which is long overdue in racing. Lincoln graduated from the University of Montana and is studying to be a veterinarian and Harriet was born in Nigeria and came to the United States as a toddler with her parents who are both petroleum engineers."

"I have heard of them, but I have been so crazy busy with that which we are forbidden to talk about that I haven't followed up and now they are honorary members of our team. I'd love to meet them."

"I smell a story brewing," Olivia quips.

"That's this week's special coffee blend. I didn't know if you might need a cup before the reception. It is a light roast with a hint of citrus," Li says.

"You could be their spokesperson. And I would love a cup. Jump starts the gray matter," I reply.

"It's way too late for that my love." Chief Detective Nederfield can be so mean. It does get a chuckle from Li and Jung.

"A cup of steaming java, as good as promised, a splash of water upon my face, a change of shirts, into our team Tessa/Kim dress Oxfords, and I am ready for a cold beer and some relaxation.

Crew Chief Tim and Chief Mechanic Peter greet us as we enter a pavilion sized tent. Our rookie driver who has already qualified for the playoffs and two new faces rush over. I note that they are all wearing Tessa/Kim crew shirts, matching blue jeans and the ubiquitous baseball cap.

"Hey boss," young Donald shouts, "I'd like you to meet our new team mates, Lincoln and Harriet. Guys, this is our team owner and world famous automotive journalist, Thomas Ballard, and the loveliest chaperone in the world." Don gives Olivia a kiss on the cheek. I think he is showing off—just a wee bit.

"Wow, I've heard so much about you." Lincoln Taylor extends his hand to shake, but then settles for an elbow bump.

"Half the things you've heard are lies and the other half are probably true." I try to paraphrase Yogi Berra—unsuccessfully.

"We are honored," the diminutive Miss Ubana says.

"We have been hearing about you, too," Olivia inserts. "Starting in the top twenty is no small effort."

"Mr. Tim, Senor Peter and Don have given us a whole new approach." The afore named three nod ever so slightly.

"On how to get the maximum from our cars and on how we should enter and exit corners, find opportunities to pass and know when to chill. I really can't believe that Don is a rookie like us."

I love the kids' enthusiasm.

"You two have good teachers and don't let anyone tell you otherwise. Results count." Li Chin is the second prettiest chaperone—and cheerleader.

"Let us all partake in the evening's activities, but remember you must be prepared mechanically and mentally when the green flag falls." Jung Kim has spoken.

We mix and mingle.

"I'm glad that Don has teammates and seems to have taken to mentoring them. It's cute how they look up to him but he is probably only a year older." Olivia has always acted maternally toward Don.

"And we know how important a year can be," I reply. Olivia raises an eye brow and punches me in the arm— lightly. I am always being abused.

CHAPTER TWENTY-ONE

The race could not have been any better. Kim's team was flawless. Even when changing four tires, they were at least a second and a half faster than the next fastest team. That doesn't seem like much, but it may make the difference in starting on the first or second rows, as opposed to the tenth row. That's how important pit stops have become. Changing only three times during the entire race was certainly a factor. The jack man nearly fell asleep between pit stops. The 31, 44, and 89 also got superior gas mileage and were able to eliminate two fuel stops. Crew Chief Tim estimated that the cars shod with Kim tires saved over three minutes on pit lane between the actual pit stop and the time spent reducing speed and then getting up to speed again. Folks, that's almost two free laps!

The three cars ran flawlessly although the Camaro definitely had a speed advantage. Don won another race, but was almost gathered up in a crash near the end of the race. A number of seasoned drivers clearly were feeling the pressure and made moves that they might never had considered except for the steadiness of the 31. Lincoln, who had never finished above 20th on the Trophy circuit, came in a very credible twelfth while Harriet finished ninth—the first top ten finish for a woman since Danika. Jung Kim and I spent about four minutes in the winner's circle. Not only were we trying to avoid the press, present company excluded, but it was Don's time in the lime light. I was sure that questions were going to come fast and furious about the performance of Kim tires and we agreed to let Peter Coroletti answer their questions—in Italian. Tim Sun followed our lead, quickly fled and went back to the rigs to load the cars. Apparently the 44 and 89 were going to be stabled in Palm Beach.

Olivia, Li, Jung, and I quick step it back to the RV.

"Gottcha!" A voice shouts.

Charlie White, one of the old school members of the Fourth Estate is standing in front of us with his cell phone/camera.

"You idiot," I yell. "You'll never get a decent picture with your fat finger in front of the lens."

"I hate these things. How are you Thomas? And Olivia, are you still with this underworked and overpaid slob?"

"Charlie, why aren't you working? Like getting an interview or something?"

"Why? When I have a chance to meet my hero, Jung Kim. Sir, you have turned the sport up side down . . . all for the better. Kudos."

"Jung, Li, this creature in Charlie Henderson. Two time Pulitzer award winning journalist, who is one of my oldest friends and one of the only writers I know who can be trusted to keep his word."

"I may faint after such accolades."

Both Jung and Li bow.

"Charlie, what are you doing here? This is not exactly your beat." I ask.

"Can you get me into the event next Monday at Palm Beach?"

"To the point. I won't ask your source unless you say it's a creepy guy with a fake British accent who wears a white suit at the track."

"Actually, I haven't heard a word from our friend Comrade Shaw in well over a month. It comes from the Beltway."

"Mr. Kim, I am aware of your relationship to the track at Gold Coast, to Kim Enterprises and to everyone trying to keep the G-7 *show and tell* safe and a secret. Thomas, I just want to be there. No cell phone, no camera, no pencil or notebook."

"Charlie, what's the hook?"

"Basically, I have stage 4 pancreatic cancer and I have always been the reporter on the outside. I just want to stand around and take it all in. Seriously. No bullshit."

His normally bright laser sharp eyes look dull and sad. I don't want to end up like Charlie. I guess "owning" a NASCAR team has, virtually over night, made me an insider, but I get it.

"It's not our call, but we will give it a try." I try to sound cheerful.

"Despite what everyone says, you are a good egg." Charlie smiles gives me a bump fist, blows a kiss to Olivia, places his hands, somewhat shakily, on his knees and bows to Jung and Li and then turns and walks away.

"I do not understand. Your friend just called you an egg," Jung Kim says.

"It's actually a term of endearment. I wish we could do something. Charlie is not a mere journalist, he is a news reporter. He will dig and dig until he finds answers. His writing style is eloquent."

"I have an idea," Li Chin begins. "I need someone who can help me with press releases and basic public relations. Let's retain his services effective immediately and after the event, we can talk about the future."

"I don't think he has a lot of future. I think we have to deal with the immediate present," Olivia replies.

Jung Kim nods to his wife. "Put him on the Kim Enterprises employee list and make sure you send his information to that Agent Driver fellow for vetting."

"Thank you," I add.

"In Korean we have a word for a good deed, it's doing a mitzvah."

"Jung, how long have you been in Palm Beach?" I ask.

"A little too long, since I am already confusing Korean and Yiddish." His smile is infectious. The guy has a great sense of humor.

"Let's pack up, try to congratulate back to back winner Donald Montgomery and head over to the airport. We have a long week in front of us. I think that a glass of champagne is in order, *n'est pas?*" Both Li Chin and Jung Kim are on a roll.

"I am going to visit the track's world famous showers and freshen up. I want to change shirts in case someone gets close to me."

"Shall I alert the press?" Olivia adds sarcastically.

"Stealing lines from my favorite movie . . . for shame."

"Just hurry up. I want to give our number one driver a big hug." Olivia really cares for the kid.

"Fleet of foot, I am." I go into the RV and retrieve a clean shirt, a towel, my shaving kit and dash off to the showers.

"He must keep you amused," Li says.

"Oh he does, but only for short periods of time."

"I heard that!"

"Just move it mister. You got four minutes before we start on the champagne."

"I cannot believe you two have been together for only two years. You sound like we do and what's it been . . . over twenty years?" Jung shakes his head.

"And you have loved every moment." Li gives Jung a kiss.

"I saw that!" I quickly retreat into the showers.

After a little post race press conference, we say our farewells and head over to the airport. I think that Donald is developing a following. A lot of groupies ask for his autograph and a selfie. I can't help thinking how proud his uncle, albeit a mob member, would be. Olivia pointed out that despite his name, he is becoming the next Italian Stallion of the stock car racing circuit. Even some fans wear the red, green and white of the Italian flag. He handles all this attention with real class. Whenever someone came up to interview him, he would always introduce his teammates and of course Tim and Peter, the latter of whom would listen to a technical mechanical question in English and respond in Italian. That's Cal Tech for you.

We land in Orlando around 8 pm, after a smooth trip.

"Can we drive you somewhere?" Olivia asks.

"No, we are continuing to Palm Beach. I feel like a gypsy and want to sleep in our own bed," Li Chin answers.

"I didn't know you had a place in Palm Beach." I hope I don't sound pushy.

"We bought it about a month ago. Since we have the track here, I thought that it would make sense to buy a place. It's small and comfortable. We moved in last Monday after a bit of a decorating," Jung replies.

"Since you two will be down here starting Friday afternoon until Monday. We would love to have you stay and be our first guests. I am very proud of the make over. It is a fusion of Asian and Jimmie Buffet." Li delivers her line straight faced, while Olivia and I start laughing. "Seriously, we got three full bedroom suites and you will be comfortable." Of that, I have no doubt.

"You are too kind. We will accept only if we can get down here by noon so you and I, and hopefully Sheila, can cruise Worth Avenue."

"Jung, I think we have been out maneuvered," I suggest.

"Do not ever act surprised. Always make it seem like business as usual . . . which it is. I'll have the plane at your airport at 11."

"If we fly in your plane, can we claim mileage on our expense account?" I smile.

"Today's flight was for Kim Tire. Next Friday's flight will be for National Security, yours and ours." Jung Kim bows.

CHAPTER TWENTY-TWO

The next four days seem interminable. Meetings, calls, emails, inspections and even some complaints, but everything is basically running smoothly, at least from our point of view. The event organizers have the unenviable task of dealing with ten thousand details. Our job is just to make it safe. Sir Bertram has his side of the race card well in hand. Marshall Leventhal's group is a little more casual, but equally enthusiastic. With few exceptions, mostly teams coming from abroad, all the vintage drivers are going to spend the weekend in Palm Beach. That is good news on several fronts: they will enjoy the extra track time getting ready to put on a great show for the assembled dignitaries and it will allow the Formula E teams and the F-1 teams not traveling to the Gold Coast a less crowded paddock in which to set up.

Protocols have been initiated, tested, and well received by all. The executive orders have been put in place and there has been little resistance, especially when the alternative to non-compliance is non-attendance. When 100,000 fans descend upon Citrus Grove, there may be a wrinkle or two, but the first two days will have smaller crowds so any tweaking needed can be completed before the influx starting

Thursday. The track has provided that private auto parking will be scheduled according to seat location so that everyone does not arrive at once—hopefully.

By noon on Friday, both Olivia and I are ready for a change in venues. We are whisked down to Palm Beach by the Kim rent-a-jet. Lu Chin meets us in a company Suburban and tells us that we are to meet his sister and brother-in-law at Guido's, Palm Beach's best Italian seafood restaurant. Why not?

The building looks like the Amalfi coast has moved to south Florida. The view features the breaking surf of the Atlantic but the charm and ambiance of the Mediterranean. Our host and hostess greet us as we enter. The ladies exchange distance kisses, while Jung and I elbow bump.

"This place is very cool," I whisper to Olivia.

"There are some people I would like you to meet," Jung Kim announces.

As we approach our table, a beautiful raven haired woman, almost as tall as Olivia and Li, begins to rise as her companion holds her chair.

"Francesca, Marco Marcello, I would like you to meet our team owner, Thomas Ballard and the lovely Olivia Nederfield."

"It is long overdue. You have done so much for young Donello and we are so proud of his accomplishments," Marco says in very heavily accented Italian.

"He is a wonderful boy and speaks of you both as his family," Francesca adds.

I quickly compose myself and reply, "He is a pleasure to be with, both as a driver and as a compassionate human being."

"Things have not been easy for him and we have tried to make sure that he has opportunities to find his calling, preferably not in the family business." Marco chortles. "Needless to say, having the privilege of sponsoring him is a great honor. And now I understand that we may have some new drivers. Not Italian, but nice kids."

This is like a scene from the *Godfather*, but more genuine.

"I think we should sit and order, before Thomas and Olivia pass out from hunger," Li Chen says.

A waiter hustles over and says something very quietly in Italian to Senor Marcello, who simply nods.

"*Molto bene*," he says and the waiter withdraws. "I have taken the liberty of ordering for all of us. A little of everything. And some wine."

"Marco loves this restaurant," Francesca explains. "Actually he owns the restaurant. We have a place in Fort Lauderdale where we spend the winters, but we come here at least once a week."

Why not, if you own the place?

"Marco and I wanted to get together with you about plans for our team . . . your team," Jung Kim says.

"If anything, it is our team. I couldn't have done this without your help," I respond.

"Kim Tires would never have been able to showcase its tires without you. What would you think if we hired Lincoln and Harriet for the Trophy circuit and also Chad Collins to the Junior circuit for a limited number of races? He should continue his studies in computer engineering on a scholarship from Kim Enterprises. Carlos will remain as is until he shows me that he has the mental acumen to be a world class driver."

"I will have to open more pizza restaurants, but we like the idea, as long as the cars remain red, green, and white." That brings a bit of mirth to the group. "My English may not be too good, but I understand business and diversity is the future."

"I am overwhelmed. Our infrastructure will have to grow exponentially. We will need new cars for next year and a lot of personnel, including chassis designers, engine builders . . . the list goes on."

"Thomas, do not worry. Marco's family owns forty Ford dealerships and that should give us some leverage. Also, Kim Tires is prepared to offer Ford a very attractive price to put our tires as original equipment on their performance vehicles. We have access to the finest engineers in the world. We can use Gold Coast as our headquarters and if you want a dyno, we will install a dyno. If you want a wind tunnel, we will install a wind tunnel. Our technology will be applied to every component of the car's design. I am already putting pressure on the powers to be, to allow, three Tessa/Kim cars to use our tires for the entire year. That will be the only way to evaluate our performance and safety."

"And Peter Corolatti can get some of the world's finest mechanics to work for us. Believe me," Marco adds.

I believe him. Before I can comment, food by the platter arrives, together with several bottles of wine which Marco examines, nods and then tastes. I feel like I am free falling.

Everything is perfect. Conversation includes literature, music, and of course, food.

"Francisca, Marco, *grazie*. It was perfect. However, we need to check in at the track," Olivia says.

"*Si*, you have a very important job the next few days," Marco responds.

How does he know? Jung Kim wouldn't say anything.

"Thomas, you have a puzzled look. The Italian ambassador to the United States is my cousin," Francesca announces. "He will be at the conference."

I guess *a secret once shared is no longer a secret.* I make an executive decision. I am not going to address expanding our team until I run everything by the Bentley Seven plus one. They will be arriving tomorrow morning. I am going to suggest to Olivia and then to the entire team, that they are briefed about all the security and health protocols. They are the best of the best and not to seek their input would be foolish.

CHAPTER TWENTY-THREE

After a quick drive to the track, I ask for a general meeting. Olivia, Elias, Jung, and I address the gathered troops. "The first wave of cars will begin arriving at 8 o'clock tomorrow morning. Chief Detective Nederfield, Sheriff Rosewood, Director White, Mr. Kim, and I expect to be at the track by 7, since it is my experience, especially with the vintage drivers, that earlier means better. Coffee and donuts will be waiting at the base of the start/finish line. Each team will be assigned a paddock. There aren't enough garages for everyone, so we have decided to reserve them for the F-1 participants. They're used to getting the red carpet treatment. The vintage folks are just plain happy to be here." That's gets a chuckle from the crowd.

I pass the microphone to Elias. "Please make sure you all follow the protocols for health and safety. Bring your IDs. Those of you, who have been pre-approved to carry fire-arms, please arrive fifteen minutes early with your weapon unloaded. Secret Service Agent Driver and Deputy Silver will check you and your weapon against the master list. Everyone will be required to pass through the same security as the participants. TSA Director White will also have bomb sniffing dogs at the screening machines." Elias passes the microphone to Olivia.

"All of you will be subject to health checks each day. If any of you does not feel 100%, please let us know. We will have random COVID testing throughout the event. For those of you going to Citrus Grove, we will be repeating the same procedure. If anyone has any question or sees anything out of the ordinary, I want you to immediately ask or report it to any of the four of us, Agent Driver, Agent Forbes, or Deputy Silver." She hands the microphone to Jung Kim.

"Good afternoon. My name is Jung Kim. I have not had the pleasure meeting all of you but I want to welcome you to Gold Coast Raceway. In addition to being the guy from Kim Tires, together with my wife Li Chin and her brother Lu Chin, who I am sure you have seen around and recognize as our own *Incredible Hulk*, we are handling the electronic surveillance monitoring devices and communications. If we observe something, how do you say, fishy, we will contact one or more of you. Thank you for your efforts to make this a safe event and to create a prototype for other large venue events." Jung bows to the crowd and returns the microphone to me.

"Are there any questions?" I ask the crowd. No response. "When you are done with whatever it is that you were doing before I dragged you away, call it a day. We will all be putting in a lot of hours the next few days. Before you all feel sorry for yourselves, a lot of us have to do this again starting Tuesday." That gets a lot of hisses and boos, which quickly changes to clapping.

As the crowd disperses, I turn to my colleagues. Any comments?

"You speak too quickly," Olivia comments. "But the gist was okay."

"I think you need to work on your hand gestures," Elias adds.

I give him one of my specials. Everyone starts to laugh. "Three years of method acting at University of Florida is responsible." It's the best I could come up with.

"Maybe you should consider a tuition refund." Even Jung Kim gets into the barrage of criticisms at my expense.

"It'll be alright, sweetie. I will still love you." Olivia gives me a smooch. The others give me a round of applause.

Lu Chin drives the four of us back into downtown Palm Beach. He stops at a twelve story building with an ocean view where a doorman greets us. Olivia and I travel light, so I throw the flight bag over my shoulder and follow our host and hostess to the twelfth floor. No surprise and it is breathtaking. After we bank our first ten million or so, I want to hire Li Chen to decorate our house. Not that Olivia wouldn't do a great job and I'd always know where to hang my body armor, but the condo is magnificent, from the vista including the ocean, to the melding deep turquoise blue and gold. Truly the Orient meets Margaretville. Jung Kim's penchant for understatement is the only way one can describe their unit as small, unless everything in Palm Beach is over the top, which is a possibility. Because tomorrow will begin early and end late, Li Chin suggests we eat light and retire early. Music to my ears.

Eating light is like *we have a small condo*. Soup, salad with shrimp on a bed of rice pasta, and a fruit plate with cheese is hardly a light fare. Scrumptious, yes. Our bed has been turned down since we put our travel bag on the folding mahogany luggage rack. How did that happen? I never saw anyone enter or leave the unit. It's not important. A hot shower is important and so is a good night's sleep.

We lay out our clothes for tomorrow: chinos, comfortable sneakers, and green polo type shirts with a sheriff's badge embroidered on the left pocket, and our last name on the right. No rank. We decide to bring our Team Bentley shirts for the evening's activities, which have not actually been planned. We promised the caterer we'd give her a head count by noon. I think hamburgers, cheeseburgers, hot dogs, potato salad, and coleslaw is the perfect Saturday night at the race track meal. Mustn't forget ice cold beer. Probably wine as well. If we get a couple of late arrivals, they will be easy to accommodate.

We leave for the track a little after 6 o'clock. Lu Chin is waiting for the four of us downstairs. Either he gets up very early, or as I suspect, stays in yet another bedroom. We each have a mug of steaming Columbian java to start the day. I wonder if the name *java* comes from the place name which is known for its wonderful coffee.

It takes less than fifteen minutes to reach the track. I guess the residents of Palm Beach are still sleeping at six in the morning on a Saturday. When we pull up to the front entrance I notice that a trailer, flanked by two RVs, is already parked in the paddock.

"What the hell?" I mutter. Then I take a second look. The 36 foot enclosed trailer is painted a very familiar shade of British Racing Green emblazoned with a yellow **B**, which explains who the early bird is, but not how they got into the secured paddock. Elias and I are going to have a heart to heart.

"Is that who I think it is?" Olivia says a little too loudly.

"I hope you don't mind. I got a text from Hans Leiter last night saying that they had made fantastic time getting down here and could they get in a little early. If it was anyone else, I would have said no, but . . ." Jung Kim replies.

"Understood. Hard to say no to that group," I respond.

Lu Chin delivers us to the start/finish line just as Sheriff Rosewood approaches with the Bentley gang. Each carries a green Bentley mug.

"Olivia, Thomas so good to see you," chef extraordinaire Stanford shouts. We are immediately swamped by our friends.

Mother Superior Margaret gives us each a kiss and says, "*Bonjour*, I so glad to see you, although we knew you would be here making everything safe. Well almost everything."

"Thomas, I was given a check list of almost a dozen security glitches," Elias says.

Hans Leiter shrugs. "It is a very small list considering how much you had to do in so little time. Jung Kim sent us the security specifications and asked us to review all the precautions. We arrived early evening and looked for anything obvious. Frederick and Cecil ran a series of scans and everything worked well. We wanted to run laser checks as soon as it got dark. Pierre was able to scale the fence at turn six and walk undetected to the edge of the track. The beam coverage lapse is small, but it creates vulnerability. It is simply a matter of re-aiming the laser. Li Chin, your open communication channel can be accessed for almost two miles. It is not a real security issue, unless you have an emergency and cannot switch frequency."

Why is it I always feel so awestruck by these folks? Because they are the best.

"I took heat vision images of each building on the grounds and found several areas that are potential problems," Charles Llewellyn, world famous photographer adds. There are crawl spaces above both the bath facilities and three large concessions stands which could provide shelter for someone up to no good. Franco came up with a quick and easy solution, Kevlar cloth."

"*Sì.* By blocking the entrance to each, what we call, cubby holes, with the fabric, entrance would be very difficult. Mini battery powered movement activated cameras could transmit to your security monitors. *Questo é tutto.* That's it. Hans?"

"A very short list, *n'est pas?*" Hans inserts.

"*Mes amis*, we did not want to butt in, but Sheriff Rosewood asked Jung Kim to have us double check. It is a very important assignment and added on top of the race next week, another pair . . . actually sixteen eyes might just be of assistance." Margaret is so classy.

"Elias, I suspect you've been talking to Mike about our friends from Team Bentley," Olivia observes.

"Before you ask, we did the same review at Citrus Grove late yesterday and early last night before we headed to Palm Beach." Cecil and his brother Charles are proud of themselves—deservedly. "We gave the list to Sheriff McCarthy who was with us. It is very short.

"Since I don't need the extra calories, I am by-passing donuts and will send out Charlie, who has been a great help, and a technician over to the fence this morning and get maintenance to procure and install the Kevlar fabric and wireless cameras. The idea to secure the crawl space is excellent since we will be testing a lot of technology and corporate espionage is not unheard of." Jung Kim bows and he and Li Chin begin to walk toward the large garage housing Kim headquarters until the new facility is completed.

If I was paranoid, I might find a conspiracy theory in the fact that neither Olivia nor I were a party to either surprise inspection.

"You were intentionally excluded from our efforts, not because you weren't thorough, but because you two are very thorough. We didn't want you obsessing about what you had forgotten. As you see, everything was *très bon*." I think Margaret could calm down a charging rhino.

I hold up my coffee cup. "I need a refill and a couple of donuts."

"You may have one more cup of coffee and one donut," Olivia announces, bringing gales of laughter.

CHAPTER TWENTY-FOUR

I am overwhelmed and relieved. I guess I am a little pleased as well. We've done well.

"Thomas, you are talking to yourself," Olivia observes.

"Was I coherent?"

"About the same as always . . . somewhat. Having Team Bentley on board is such a relief. I feel like pressure of the unknown has been all but extinguished. All we have is the *x-factor* which is not something we can anticipate or control, but simply contain and react.'"

"Well said. I am a little bummed out that I didn't think about the crawl spaces. It would be easy for someone to enter the facilities over the weekend and store the components of a weapon which could then be assembled, used, and disassembled."

"Sweetie, no one else thought about it either." Chief Detective Nederfield tries to make me feel better. She succeeds.

"There must be some super karma that keeps those folks in our lives." I don't believe in a lot of supernatural interventions, but Team Bentley comes close—real close. I take a sip of my newly refreshed cup of coffee, which I don't remember pouring.

"What kind of donut do you want . . . glazed or cake?" Olivia brings me back into the here and now.

"Thomas, try the blueberry cake donut," Franco yells. "It is almost as good as Stanford's muffins, but not quite." I think the second comment was made because the team chef was standing less than two feet away.

"Saved yourself old man, but it is very good. I will have to get Sheriff Elias to introduce me to the talent which runs the bake shop. Swap recipes." We all laugh, including Franco.

I see Cecil engaged in conversation with a rather tall, thin man, who I do not recognize. Since I am in charge of credentials and the track isn't supposed to be open for another forty minutes, I think I will stroll over.

Cecil turns to me and says, "Bard Ballard, I want you to meet the fearless leader of us old farts who race old cars, Marshall Leventhal."

"My pleasure and thank you for all your help." I look out toward the paddock and do not see any other trailers.

"Can't get in until 8 o'clock I was told. No exceptions unless of course you are one of the *Incredible Eight*." His comments are made with respect not sarcasm. "I've been told that both facilities have passed their tech inspection." Marshall winks.

I don't want to go too far along the path I see before me so I switch subjects adroitly. Speaking of tech inspection, how are the vintage racers addressing the issue?"

"I should know better than to bait an esteemed member of the fourth estate into a conversation he would rather not have."

Cecil, Marshall, and I are joined by Frederick and Charles. "Sorry for eavesdropping, but I am rather proud of our inspection process. Cecil designed the software. Every car that competes with us is entered into our data base, including technical specifications, photographs, and safety measures. Every lap from every timed practice session or race is entered for each car. Any mishaps are entered. It's like an electronic log book. At each event, the car and safety equipment is visually inspected and the results logged. Each car undergoes an annual inspection, which is rather meticulous, emphasizing safety rather than authenticity. The cars must fall within the spirit of vintage racing, but we do not get into details like the firewall on the Type 123 should be red and not gray. The inspectors are very experienced. The system works. Since vintage race cars are by their nature expensive and since everyone is pretty much self-financed and the only trophy awarded each weekend is for bragging rights until the next weekend, everyone is on their best behavior."

"Fantastic. Why isn't your design used by the other race organizations?" I ask.

"As soon as Frederick finishes his field trials, we will," Cecil answers.

"You mean as soon as the patents are issued," Marshall Leventhal inserts.

"That hurts," I add.

"Yes, but accurate," Frederick responds. "We have all been fortunate in our endeavors in the private sector and now we can create something that we can share with those who love automotive racing. The program is being modified to work with Li Chin's testing model. We see the technology as a breakthrough in safety research. We have agreed to create a foundation to fund educational opportunities for the new generation. We will assign the patents and deposit any licensing fees into an account. We are hoping you and Olivia will join our board. Actually, we figured each of you is a *two for*."

A two for?" I ask.

"Two for the price of one. Olivia will represent community based law enforcement and help recruit young women for the program. We weren't so sure about you," Cecil pauses to judge my reaction. "But since you are a reasonably erudite member of the automotive press, a team owner and a pretty good detective, we thought we would take a chance." Cecil starts to laugh and is immediately joined by Frederick.

Marshall Leventhal shakes his head and says, "Since I have to put up with these two, I am going to get a cup of coffee, return to my trailer and drive through the fence if they won't let me in."

"I didn't mention the laser system which surrounds the track. If you break the beam thousands of tiny paint balls are instantly released. Your trailer would be a cross between Jackson Pollack and a first grade finger painting." I try to maintain a straight face, except that if the beam is broken, bad things actually will happen. I look at my watch and breathe a sign of relief. It's 7:45 am.

"Your coffee my dear . . . and a donut." Olivia hands me a steaming mug and a half a donut. "The blueberry cake donut is really quite good."

"I think I will grab a donut with my coffee and then make sure no one tries to sneak ahead of me. See you later . . . at tech inspection." Marshall is really a good sport and has really organized the vintage program. I glance over toward the gate. I count fourteen trailers, plus two factory Ferrari tractor-trailers followed by two motor homes, all sporting the prancing stallion.

I never thought we could pull this off.

CHAPTER TWENTY-FIVE

By 10 o'clock, over thirty vintage racing teams have been assembled in the paddock as well as six F-1 teams. Having Elias' green uniformed deputies direct traffic is a lot more efficient than the loosey goosey approach one usually sees at a race. Tech inspection is proceeding quickly and it looks like the track will open for the first session by a little after noon—ahead of schedule. Jung Kim has six midnight blue KIA K-5s in front of his temporary headquarters. These cars are obviously tricked out. Gadgets and gizmos are attached everywhere. Several Formula One drivers, clutching their helmets and gloves are hovering around these high tech wonders obviously waiting for a ride.

"Did you order the weather especially for the event?" Sir Bertram's voice is unmistakable.

"I thought you were going to visit Harry Potter," I shout over the noise of the 4.5 liter Alfetta's, the V16 BRMs, and even the Offenhauser Indy type engine.

"The wife thought that a day of shopping would be far superior to a day at the Magic Kingdom, which I assured her would be open next week. Looks like everything is going along splendidly. I saw Dr. Voss and his newly restored British racing green Connaught. He and Cecil Llewellyn have designed the most marvelous software for examining cars for safety and technical compliance. FIA wants to license their program. And look, they've brought along the Talbot Lago T26C. What a magnificent machine. I wonder who is going to drive. The Bentley folks list everyone as a potential driver on their application. They all have the requisite licenses."

"Except, I suspect, Margaret Leiter," Olivia inserts.

"Actually, no. Margaret holds a full competition license and has competed in many events, especially rallyes over the years, with great success I might add. Hans does the navigating, but Margaret drives."

"I guess I am not surprised." I want to ascertain how much Sir Bertram knows about Team Bentley, but we are interrupted by Charlie Henderson skidding to a stop in a golf cart.

"Thomas, Olivia, please come quickly. There has been an incident at turn six. We were going over to realign the laser and saw a body. Quite dead." Charlie is going to have a stroke if he doesn't slow down.

"Charlie, how do you know he's dead?" Olivia asks. "And how do you know it's a *he*?"

After several deep breaths, Charlie responds. "Detective Nederfield, as a beat reporter for forty years, I've seen my share of dead people and when a person is lying on his back with a bright red spot in the middle of his chest, it usually isn't good. I left one of Jung's guys to watch the body and make sure no one touches it and then high tailed it back here."

As I turn toward Olivia, she is already on her cell. She mouths the word *Elias*. I nod. Suddenly another golf cart appears. Franco is at the wheel. Charles Llewellyn is sitting next to him with a brace of cameras around his neck. Hans, with his lap top open, sits in the back next to Sheriff Rosewood, whose cell is ringing. Olivia hangs up.

"We'll get in the cart with Charlie," I announce.

"I've called the ME," Elias says. "I was with Agent Driver when Mr. Leiter called a few minutes ago. He is getting Forbes to send a couple of folks to the outside access point of the track near the incident. He will wait for the ME. No flashing lights or siren. Just a casual look-see."

Hans looks up from his screen and says, "Frederick, Cecil, and Pierre are taking the other cart to pick up Jung Kim and drive the track counterclockwise and meet us. Margaret and Stanford are setting up the RV for whatever is needed."

I am getting a pit in the bottom of my stomach. I should have had the second donut. "X-factor?" I whisper to Olivia, as Charlie Henderson puts the pedal to the medal.

"I am having the same thought." Chief Detective Nederfield and I both stroke our chin and wait for the cart to race around the track.

We do not generate much attention since almost everyone is otherwise checking over their cars. Fortunately the FBI agents are wearing race track clothing as opposed to suits, so they blend into the crowd. We arrive an instant before Elias, Hans, Franco, and Charles, the latter making us all stand at least twenty feet away from the scene so he can photograph everything. Elias and Hans put on surgical gloves and approach the dead man, obviously Asian, obviously dead with a large red stain on his previously white Kim Tire shirt. Sheriff Rosewood raises his hand for everyone to stop.

"Something is wrong," Elias says.

Duh, there's a dead man lying on the ground.

The Sheriff leans over the corpse and sniffs. I am not kidding, but then again, Elias is 'Glades born and raised. Hans seems to understand. He quickly removes a Q-tip from his kit and dabs a sample of the blood, which he smells and hands to Elias who says, "This is not blood. It is paint from a paint ball gun."

Blow me over with a feather. Could Li Chin's *x-factor* exercise have gone terribly wrong?

"Deputy Ballard," A voice calls from the fence line. "Nothing out of the ordinary on this side of the track. No tire tracks or obvious signs of trampled grass. The fence links are in tact. Should we go back and report to Agent Forbes?"

"If you don't mind, stand at ready. This is not as simple as it appears. I don't want word to get out, but if some curiosity seeker or more importantly paparazzi get near, secure both the person and any cameras." I hope my *I'm in charge* voice sounds convincing. Truth be told, I am as confused as the next guy, or girl, as the case may be.

The second Team Bentley golf cart approaches. Jung Kim looks real unhappy. He literally leaps out before the cart stops and runs up toward the body.

"His name was Lin Soo. He is a member of the Korean diplomatic corps. He is an old friend of ours and was helping my wife plan some surprises for you. How did this happen?" I can tell Jung Kim is upset. Although his manner is calm, he is talking about twice as fast as normal 7for him.

"Jung, it is not as it appears. When Mr. Henderson said he found a dead body with what appeared to be a large chest wound, we assumed he had been shot. Sheriff Rosewood was skeptical and he and I have confirmed that the apparent wound is red paint from a paint ball gun and certainly not fatal. He died of another cause. I need your permission,

Sheriff Rosewood, and also your permission Jung to examine the body. I am not sure when your medical examiner will arrive but I want to take body temperature readings to I can establish time of death. I also want Charles to photograph the victim." Hans Leiter has set up the investigation parameters.

Pierre has taken some orange cones from the back of the cart and begins to set up a work area four paces from the body.

"I think I had better tell Sheila what is happening," Olivia suggests.

"Please wait until we have a little more information. Her absence might raise suspicions. We have already contaminated the ground immediately around the body. I have asked Stanford to spread the word that we have been given permission to drive around the track in our golf carts to familiarize ourselves with the layout and that the track owner has offered that anyone who wants to tour the track in a cart, on foot, or by bicycle, may sign up. Groups will be released starting at 11:30 in fifteen minute intervals. That gives us less than a half hour to do what we need to do."

"Who is that?" Charlie Henderson whispers to Olivia and me.

"Don't ask!" We reply together. "Just listen and do what you are told."

Pierre shoos everyone back outside his orange cones, except Hans and Charles. Frederick and Cecil are walking around with handheld devices, which give off a faint beeping sound. Franco retrieves a blue tarp from the back of one of the carts and places it next to the body onto which he places Hans' laptop and what looks like an old fashion doctor's bag. Hans removes a portable digital temperature scanner. Franco key strokes something into the laptop and suddenly an outline of a generic body appears. Hans takes a series of readings beginning at the head of the former Lin Soo. The temperature then appears on the monitor's image. Scanning takes almost five minutes. Hans then takes out a probe and attaches to the digital thermometer. He measures the soil temperature which appears on the monitor. Charles concentrates on the victim's head and upper torso. I think they want to reposition the body but patiently wait for the ME, who arrives in a Kim Tire ATV driven by Li Chin."

After introductions are exchanged, the ME, Dr. Jacobson, a mid 50s athletic type, looks like he just got pulled off a golf course, which he probably did. His shoes give him away. Maybe the glove in the back pocket, too.

He and Hans go into conference, while Frederick and Cecil report that they have found no chemical residue from a weapon; no breaks of any kind in the beams that have been installed along the perimeter; or any sound transmitting device, which I later learn might emit waves that can cause death. Basically nothing.

"Thomas, do you think that Mr. Soo might have had a heart attack?" Olivia asks.

I look over my shoulder and see Franco, Hans and Dr. Jacobson gently move the body onto the tarp. More pictures. Elias walks over and asks, "Do you think he could have died of natural causes, like a heart attack?"

"I just asked the same thing. I guess we won't know until we get the autopsy report," Olivia ponders.

"Knock, knock! We have the leaders of the free world here in less than two days and don't know the cause of death. That is serious shit we are in." I hope I don't sound too dramatic.

"We actually know the cause of death with a high degree of certainty." Dr. Jacobson's voice is rather high pitched for a man of his size.

"The body does not appear to have any visible signs of trauma, except for some tissue swelling around the heart. At first it appeared that Mr. Soo could have actually died from the paint ball. It is entirely possible that Li Chin's charade actually exacerbated some pre-existing condition, but the ball actually struck the victim in his upper right shoulder. The paint splattered toward the center of the chest." Hans sounds like a medical school professor. Like how should I know?

"So the paint ball had nothing to do with Lin Soo's death?" I think I've been listening.

"Correct. The body temperature readings make it clear that death was virtually instantaneous and within the last hour or slightly less. You've heard the expression *dead before he hit the ground*? Also the incident was massive. No bluing of the lips or swelling of the tongue," Dr. J reports.

"Thomas, this is not to say that we have concluded that the cause of death was natural. There are many ways in which a heart attack can be induced and that is what we need to do . . . immediately. Sheriff Rosewood, can you arrange for an ambulance to take the body to the morgue. Dr. Jacobson has asked if I can help him since my knowledge regarding these matters far exceeds his." Hans looks at our in house Nobel laureate, Frederick, whose knowledge of toxins, poisons, bacteria and viruses that can replicate a heart attack is unmatched, and nods. "Dr. Voss will be joining us."

"I suggest that the track EMT vehicle be dispatched. It is far less conspicuous," Jung Kim, who has his arm around Li Chin, says.

I walk over to the three FBI agents standing outside the fence, just out of ear shot. "False alarm. The guy had a massive heart attack. He was a heavy smoker. The ME is taking him to the morgue. Standard Operating Procedure. Can you give Forbes a call so he can stop holding his breath?" That gets a little laugh from the agents and gets them out of our hair.

"Thomas!" Olivia is standing next to Charlie Henderson. Actually she is holding him up.

"What's up?" I ask.

"I don't feel so good. I guess my bucket list will have to wait."

"Nonsense. You've had a little too much excitement and probably three cups of coffee on an empty stomach," Olivia says.

Charlie looks up and smiles. "Four! I knew that fourth cup was a killer, euphemistically speaking."

The EMT truck arrives. Lu Chin is driving. Lin Soo's body is placed on the gurney and loaded into the back. Hans, Frederick, and Dr. Jacobson climb in. "Two hours we will have preliminary results," Hans says.

"On a Saturday?" Dr. Jacobson asks. "How can we get all the data analyzed?"

"Don't ask!" A chorus rings out. Franco rushes up to Hans and gives him the laptop.

"I have sent the data to Margaret and it has been forwarded. The link I installed will go to the computer in the RV and will also be forwarded to those who need to know. Charles will edit and send his photos as well."

"*Tres bon.*"

"I will take Charlie back to the office. We have a place he can rest. Several of our staff are EMTs and will monitor his recovery," Li Chin says.

"Make sure I get a pretty nurse." Charlie is incorrigible.

Team Bentley, minus two, along with Jung Kim, who is giving them a guided tour of the track, head back to the paddock.

"Everything Mike has ever said about those folks is . . . a complete understatement. In less than thirty minutes we have examined the crime scene or the incident scene; ascertained cause of death; removed the body and are ready to go . . . more or less. And no one is the wiser." The Sheriff of Palm Beach County has been introduced to the *don't ask* gang.

"Let's get back. I have to go to the men's room!"

"Now that you mention it," our indigenous Sheriff adds.

"I'll drive. You two try and hold it until we get back to the paddock." Olivia is all heart. I resist the urge to laugh.

CHAPTER TWENTY-SIX

After all these years of going to car races, you would expect the sights and sounds of prerace warm-up to be rather ordinary. Not so. What appears to be chaos is in fact a choreographed ballet of machines. The cars are lined up ready to enter the Coliseum. The contrast between the sleek high tech Formula One cars and the *mano y mano* front engine fire burners is something books are written about.

I notice that most of the drivers are taking advantage of Jung Kim's offer to tour the track. Once again the contrast, then and now, is apparent. The F-1 teams look like they are competing in the Tour d' France, mounting bicycles and wearing Spandex, while the vintage drivers seek refuge in golf carts which would put the best The Villages has to offer to shame. That's a Central Florida insider's joke.

As the last of the golf carts return to the paddock, I see Franco emerge from the RV wearing a black driver's suit with red, green, and white epaulettes and a helmet air brushed to represent the Italian flag. At the same time Pierre emerges from the other RV wearing a black driver's suit with blue, red, and white epaulettes and coordinating helmet design of the French flag. They stand between the Frederick's Connaught, which Franco will drive and the beautiful Gallic Talbot. They modestly bow to one another. Everyone who is not otherwise engaged begins to applaud. The two salute as if they were WWI airplane pilots, and are then bundled into the cars. Charles and Cecil fasten all the safety equipment and together indicate to the crowd to cover their ears. The noise is deafening, but definitely cool. The first session is strictly to warm up the cars—and the drivers. Marshall Leventhal's Alfetta 158 leads the pack, followed by a bevy of beautiful Ferrari's, a Lancia D50, a brace of long nosed Vanwalls, several Mercedes W 196 *silver bullets*, a batch of BRM type 25s, and even a handful of Indy Roadsters. If one is a car junky, this is like dying and going to heaven. Speaking of which, I want to talk with Li Chin to find out about Lin Soo's whereabouts immediately before Charlie tripped upon his body.

Obviously Chief Detective Nederfield and I are on the same waive length. She pulls on my shirt sleeve because normal conversation is impossible and points toward Kim headquarters. I nod.

We waive at Sheila White, who to the best of my knowledge is still out of the loop. I think Olivia agrees that we should let her deal with the screening and other security measures. We know how Soo got into the track, so it doesn't affect the security protocol.

"I want to talk to Li Chin. We need to develop a time line." Olivia quick walks toward the Kim garage.

"Agreed. It also gives us a chance to check on Charlie."

For a temporary facility, the amount of electronic equipment is very impressive. Actually, it looks like Elon Musk did the decorating. We observe Li moving from computer monitor to computer monitor. Some are real time images of different parts of the track and some are data screens flashing numbers every nano-second.

"Olivia, Thomas, I am glad you are here. First of all, Mr. Henderson is resting comfortably in the back room. I think your diagnosis of too much caffeine is spot on. One of Sheriff Rosewood's deputies is with him. She is very pretty." We all laugh.

"Li Chin, I need to establish a chronology from the time Mr. Soo first arrived until you last saw him." Chief Detective Nederfield is no nonsense.

"I put this together for you. It lists the time Lin Soo arrived; 06:13 and the time he and I left for turn six; 06:38. During the intervening time, we went over the *x-factor* scenario. We weren't sure how it would develop and I remember telling him that he might have to *play dead* for an hour or more. He laughed and said that he better visit the facilities since he just drank a cup of tea."

"Wait!" I think that turned too many heads. "Do you know where and when he got the tea?"

"And is there any possibility the cup is still here . . . unwashed?" Olivia adds.

"We always have a large urn of hot water and one of coffee. Lin Soo was a traditionalist and liked green tea and honey in the morning. It has only been a little over a year since Jung Kim started drinking coffee and he brings his own, as you know. Let me ask. Better yet, let us review the security video. We have several cameras covering the interior of the garage. We are not spying on our staff but are testing a new low light high definition unit which we hope to commercialize and use for public space security, like parking lots, lobbies, and large open spaces. Come."

We follow Li Chin into a room off the main garage. Eight monitors process images from the garage. Unlike most security pictures, these are in color and crystal clear. I wonder whether facial recognition software could be installed. Scary. This technology will help really law enforcement. It is so much better than the grainy images we see on TV with the announcement *if you recognize this person, call the Crime Fighter hot line.* And of course those pictures are so poor that you couldn't pick out your own brother, if you had one.

Olivia and I each pull up a chair next to Li Chin, whose fingers fly across the keyboard. Within seconds, the monitor displays images from all eight cameras, synched to each other so that each will show what ever was captured at the same time.

"The time code is at the bottom of each frame. We will start with 06:00 this morning. Several people are already in the garage. Mr. Park, who I don't think ever sleeps, is greeting personnel as they enter. He makes notes on his clip board. I will get it for you when we are done. You can see him look up at the clock when each person enters. Most everyone goes to their assigned areas and begin working. Some will pour a cup of coffee or tea. Look at the clock. It says 06:13 and Lin Soo walks in. He and Chung Park start to talk. It is not surprising since Lin Soo and Chung Park's family have been in the diplomatic corps together for years."

"There seems to be a young lady who has been hanging around the food table since we started watching. Who is she?" I ask.

"That is a very keen observation and an excellent question," Li Chin answers. "I will ask as soon as we are done."

The time code now reads 06:22 and in waltzes yours truly, Olivia, Li and Lu Chin, and Jung Kim, holding a mug.

We see Lin Soo moving toward us. The young lady who has been hovering around quickly moves toward Jung with a cup and appears to offer it to him. Jung Kim bows slightly and holds up his mug indicating he has something to drink. Lin Soo says something and points to the cup. The young lady reluctantly hands it to him. Olivia and I wave goodbye and leave the garage. Jung Kim moves toward the back of the building, stopping and talking to several people sitting at computer work stations. Li Chin, Lu Chin, and Lin Soo laugh at something and exit the building.

"My brother, Lin Soo and I went to get an ATV and drive to the far side of the track where Lu shot Lin with the paint gun, who expressed a little surprise that it felt like he had been hit with a stone. We laughed and Lin Soo lay down. I told him not to get used to sleeping on the job. Lu and I returned to the garage. I had asked Mr. Henderson to readjust the laser so I assumed he would sound the alarm as soon as he saw Lin Soo."

"I am very disturbed by one detail." Chief Detective Nederfield is going somewhere. "I missed the conversation between the young lady and Jung. Do you recall what she said, Li?"

"I wasn't really paying attention, but now that you mention it, she addressed my husband in Korean, which is discouraged, and her voice was very low both in terms of volume and pitch. It didn't register because she simply asked if Jung would like a cup of green tea and honey, which, as you know, he declined. Lin Soo said he would like a cup. The young lady stood very still until she slowly gave the cup to him."

"Thomas, are you thinking what I'm thinking?"

"I think so. A visit to Bentley headquarters is in order."

"I am not sure I fully understand," Li Chin begins. "Are you suggesting that there was something in the tea that caused Lin Soo's death and that it was really intended for Jung Kim?"

Olivia and I both shrug. "One must explore all possibilities." I don't want to paraphrase some ancient Asia proverb, but I've heard of far more outlandish possibilities.

"First things first," I begin. "We need the identity of that young lady on the security images. I would prefer to get her to a secure place to ask her some questions like how did she get into the track facility? Second, Li Chin, I think you are going to have to share this with Jung Kim and tell him not to eat or drink anything he cannot source and also make sure your brother puts together a very low key but efficient security team."

"Thomas is right. Stranger things have happened and we have seen some of them. I want to alert Hans and Frederick to the possibility that Lin Soo ingested something which may have caused his heart attack."

"So far this does not rise to the level of a high security alert. I think everything should appear normal, but I am not comfortable. I suggest a meeting with Agents Driver and Forbes, Director White, Sheriff Rosewood, you and Jung in one half hour at the big green RV with the yellow ⑧ on its side. That is where we are going."

Li Chin looks concerned—actually worried. "I will do whatever I can."

"If you find the mystery girl, bring her along. I don't have any idea if she is an amateur or a professional; is working alone or with others; or was simply trying to ingratiate herself to the boss with a cup of tea." This is not going in the direction that I had expected.

CHAPTER TWENTY-SEVEN

As we approach Team Bentley's luxurious, but functional, mobile home, both Franco and Pierre in their respective steeds pull up. Olivia and I act as pit crew, helping the obviously happy drivers out of their restraints. The same scene is being replayed by each of the vintage teams—happy drivers exiting beautiful cars.

A slightly different scene is unfolding on the false grid. Professional world class drivers are patiently waiting their turns in the blue Kim KIA K-5s. The first session for each driver will be under a full course yellow (no passing), but this should not present a problem because the pace car is a prototype KIA GT rumored to be making its debut at the 24 hours at Le Mans. These laps may be the fastest yellow on record. Our dance card does not allow for casual spectating.

Stanford opens the door as we approach with a bottle of Perrier for each of his wheel jockeys, as he calls all race car drivers. "Come inside and cool down." I think Stanford is aiming his remarks to Franco and Pierre, but we nevertheless join them.

"I am glad you are here Olivia and Thomas," Margaret says. "I just got a text from Hans that says that the death of Mr. Soo was not natural, but they haven't isolated the cause."

"We may be able to help," Chief Detective Nederfield announces and then quickly explains what we have found. It would have taken me twenty minutes to say what Olivia said in about three.

Margaret Leiter is so amazingly efficient it sometimes scares me. She writes a synopsis of Olivia's explanation-in French and sends it to Hans' email. "I have asked him to call us."

"Cecil and I are going to research various poisons which presumably have no or very little taste since Mr. Soo drank the tea without comment, although we are not even sure whether the tea was the way in which the poison was administered," Charles inserts.

"It probably is logical to first examine toxins of the Far East since there seems to be a thread," Cecil adds.

"Would anyone like some refreshments?" Stanford asks after he makes sure Franco and Pierre have finished their water.

"Aren't you looking for a needle in a haystack?" I ask Cecil.

"Actually there are only a few known plants that are real killers under the guise of heart attacks. Frederick is more versed than I am, but most poisons attack areas of the body other than cardiac, primarily through the nervous system. We have too many suppositions to formulate a strategy. Some poisons are hard to isolate in an autopsy. It is suspected that many situations in which the victim appeared to have had a heart attack are actually poisonings. I have always subscribed to the theory that if the cause of death appears fishy, it probably is."

Too many loose ends. Even if we determine the cause of death, are we any closer to determining *who* was the intended victim and *why*?

"I think we may have a possibility. At least it will help Hans narrow his focus: oleander. Although it had been suggested as a cure for Covid 19, which it is not, oleander is plentiful, deadly, and hard to detect. Unlike aconite (devil's helmet) or digitalis (foxglove), oleander has no taste or odor." Charles has projected an image of the plant which adorns almost every highway in Florida.

Margaret's cell phone rings. "*Oui?*" She listens. "Charles and Cecil seem to think that oleander may be the cause of Mr. Soo's heart attack." She listens. "I will tell them." Margaret pushes the *END* button.

Curiosity is killing me, figuratively speaking.

"Frederick had suggested several toxins, many of which are derivatives of nerium, of which oleander is one. The analysis of the stomach contents is being completed as we speak. However, Mr. Soo's blood sample show traces of VX, which is an extremely toxic synthetic chemical compound, basically a military grade nerve agent. They will be returning here shortly. The data has been sent to several sources for examination." Margaret's face shows concern.

"VX is banned by every civilized nation," Cecil exclaims.

"Wasn't Kim Jong-nam assassinated by using VX?" I ask.

"Yes," Charles replies without further comment.

"Let me briefly summarize," Olivia begins. "A South Korean national, who happens to be a member of its diplomatic corps, appears to have been murdered by ingesting oleander or VX or both. The victim drank tea which was given to him by an Asian women. The tea may have been intended for Jung Kim, a South Korean businessman and member of their intelligence community. VX was used to murder the brother of the North Korean leader Kim Jong Un."

"Too many working hypotheses," I insert. "Is there any connection to the participants at the G-7 conference? We need to connect the dots."

"*Excuse moi,*" Pierre says. "I think we may be, how do you say, spinning our wheels. Soon we will all be together. *Oui*? If we use our time to list everything we know, the others can add or delete when they get here. *N'est pas*?"

For the next twenty minutes we are confronted with how little we know. Stanford busies himself with preparing food for a dozen or so. Franco brushes out his and Pierre's driver's suits. Cecil and Charles check over the cars. Margaret is following up on the *sources* Frederick alluded to. Olivia calls her office and updates Josh. And I have a Dr. Pepper. It helps me think!

Hans and Frederick arrive first with Sheriff Rosewood. Agent Driver, who looks like death warmed over, pardon my analogy, joins us. Li Chin, Lu Chin, and Jung Kim, without the mystery tea server arrive next. Olivia's cell has a text from Agent Forbes. *Tightening perimeter—searching for girl—distributing her photo—Sheila's people are searching as well.*

"Did you get the text from Agent Forbes? I sent out an image of the young lady who served the tea to Mr. Soo to everyone," Li Chin remarks. "My brother will deal with all our employees, many of whom will feel more comfortable speaking in Korean. I was told to send a copy to Sir Bertram, who is checking with the Formula One participants and another to Marshall Leventhal."

"Both Sir Bertram and Dr. Leventhal have very high security clearances and I thought that we should close all exit routes and get as many eyes as possible looking for her." Hans is clearly team leader. "Jung Kim has opened his channels and we have sent several images to some organizations that have very accurate facial recognition software."

"We have made a tentative analysis of the cause of Lin Soo's death, but that analysis leaves more questions unanswered than answered. The heart attack was cause by a toxin found in oleander as Charles and Cecil suspected. However, a sufficient amount of VX was found to have caused death as well. Since the latter usually causes the victim to feel nauseous and often vomit, which was not apparent," Frederick dispassionately reports.

"Do you mean to say the heart attack preceded the lethal effect of VX, and that he would have died without the oleander?" I think I have it right.

"Simply said, the poor chap was murdered twice," Hans inserts.

"That is not good news because we are actually looking for two different killers who may have wanted Mr. Soo terminated for two different reasons," I conclude.

"Actually, it could have been the same murderer just making sure that Mr. Soo was going to die," Sheriff Rosewood adds.

"Or one person tried to kill Mr. Soo and the other tried to kill someone else." Chief Detective Nederfield returns us to the reality that we don't know much at all.

"We still need to ascertain whether I was an intended victim?" Jung Kim observes. "And why?"

"We need to create a chart of what we know and what we don't know," Margaret says. "I have made enquiries into Lin Soo's background. He may be a red herring."

"To divert our focus from the primary intended victim, which may not be you, Jung."

"I just had a terrible thought. What if this was simply a practice for Monday?" Everyone stares at Stanford. "Just a thought."

CHAPTER TWENTY-EIGHT

The Bentley hotel on wheels suddenly changes into a war room, complete with two large screen monitors, on which images of all the known players are projected. I think that Sheriff Rosewood is duly impressed. Well, his mouth is open, but there is no sound.

"We have displayed Lin Soo, the young lady who gave him tea, Chun Park, Charlie Henderson. These are the only subjects. There are solid red lines connecting at least one person to another and a number of blue broken lines attaching others. As we proceed through the investigation, please feel free to add subjects and connecting them to others, if possible," Hans says.

"Elias, this is the process we use . . . connect the dots," I add. "Just because someone is on the list, does not mean anything except we lack information and they seem to be on the scene."

"Hans, let's add the known facts to the graphic," Olivia suggest.

Hans makes a couple of key strokes and a time line appears. "The times are only partially complete. For example, we know when Mr. Soo entered the building, but we do not yet know when the mystery lady entered."

"We also don't know when Chun Park checked into the garage, nor Charlie Henderson. The facts may prove to be irrelevant, but they must all be ascertained." Li Chin's analytical mind is apparent. "I will have the footage from the cameras reviewed frame by frame beginning at midnight . . . earlier if necessary. Brother Lu, do you want to watch some movies with me?" Her comment gets a smile.

"Only if there's popcorn and Coke." His comment gets a laugh. "Oh I forgot where I was, I mean a Dr. Pepper." Now that gets a lot of laughs.

"Who can we get to talk to the employees, especially those who do not feel comfortable speaking English?" Jung Kim asks.

"Deputy Silver," Sheriff Rosewood inserts. "Navy Intel, graduate of the Naval language school in Monterey, speaks fluent Korean where she was stationed for three years."

"*Ma-hes hinclus, Hi-e-pas eyaha,*" I reply.

"Very good idea, Lone Wolf. Very good indeed," Hans translates.

The Palm Beach Sheriff pulls out his cell phone and speed dials his sister. They only speak a few words I understand, but Frederick inserts, "I think it best if she dresses like a civilian." Elias nods and repeats Frederick's suggestion.

"May I suggest that Chief Detective Nederfield retire to the Kim garage and have a chat with Mr. Henderson?" Margaret sounds formal. "We are preciously short of time. Jung Kim, you are probably the best to interrogate Mr. Park, *n'est pas?* When Deputy Silver arrives, we will send her to your garage."

"We will take the ATV. Li, Lu, Miss Olivia, we have much to do." Jung Kim is a man of few words. They exit the trailer.

"Thomas, would like a cup of coffee or tea?" Stanford asks. "Or even a Dr. Pepper?" Everyone appreciates the levity.

Cecil and Charles announce that the cars are ready to compete. Everything must remain as normal as possible. There are about forty minutes before the first open practice session, which has been pushed back because of the popularity of the Kim high tech car tours. I notice Marshall Leventhal waiting in line with a couple of Ferrari drivers including an absolutely gorgeous version of a young Sophia Loren in a driver's suit.

"Stanford, I'll accept a glass of unsweetened iced tea and a muffin if you have one." I'm getting hungry.

"That sounds ideal," Margaret adds. "How is the larder holding up?"

"I will place a pastry feast before your ravenous eyes in a few minutes," Chef Stanford replies.

"I will take drink orders," Franco adds. "Frederick, your driver's suit is laid out on your bed. You safety equipment is in the canvas bag. Pierre, *bon ami*, your suit is hanging in the closet and I assume your helmet and gloves are still in the Talbot."

Stanford has somehow created a platter of muffins, croissants and tiny puff pastries filled with fruit. "Please eat before we start talking about poisons."

No further invitation is required.

Our snack is interrupted almost before it begins with a series of *dings* from Hans' computer telling us that emails have been received. Frederick's computer joins the chorus, as does Olivia's cell phone.

"It's the boss," Olivia announces. "I am putting him on speaker."

"Sheriff McCarthy, so good to hear from you," I say. "Hope you are having a pleasant day away from crime solving."

"While you guys are watching car racing, I actually have a couple of armed robberies, a kidnapping and a pair of homicides to investigate without the assistance of my chief detective."

"Good day Sheriff. Actually we are in need of Miss Olivia just now," Margaret says.

"Mrs. Leiter, is my team causing a problem? I can send a cruiser to remove them." Josh is clueless about what has happened.

"From one Sheriff to another, as you can appreciate, they are integral parts of our own murder investigation," Elias adds.

"Shit! You're kidding, right?"

"Sadly, it is true and very complicated since the victim is a South Korean diplomat working with Jung Kim. The victim seems to have been killed twice." Hans is as cool as a cucumber.

"Josh, the entire group is here at Hotel Bentley waiting for forensic reports and dossiers on those already on our *connect the dots* chart." I think I just heard Josh fall over.

"Sorry for interrupting. I feel like a real idiot."

"Stanford here, Sheriff McCarthy. May I suggest a cold Dr. Pepper with a slice of lemon? We must go now. Dr. Voss is frantically signaling us. Cheers."

"The man has impeccable timing. He will probably be on his way down here in ten minutes . . . with my cousin," Sheriff Rosewood says.

"I just received the toxicology report confirming that Lin Soo had a heart attack most likely brought on by a large dose of some rather virulent oleander which is not indigenous to Florida, but can be found in the Argentinean Pampas. It was with the honey added to the tea. VX was found on the palm of the decedent's right hand, but he died before it was absorbed into his body. The application pattern suggests Mr. Soo touched some surface on which the VZ had been applied. Perhaps a doorknob or some type of handle. It did not come from the tea cup. The VX used is definitely Chinese in origin and differs from the Russian variation or the same synthetic toxin we know is possessed by Western nations, including Israel. I have shared the results with Dr. Jacobson. I am hoping to get Mr. Soo's medical records shortly to see if he had any cardiac history."

"It appears that we have no motive since we don't know whether Lin Soo was the intended victim. Maybe we should concentrate on who else might have been targeted and why." I think that Frederick's analysis is interesting but doesn't really get us anywhere. Or does it?

"May I make an observation?" Cecil Llewellyn asks. Before anyone replies, he continues. "The source of the poisons is interesting; South American and Chinese, which I assume could be Korean as well. The Korean connection is a rather complex web, but the connection to Argentina might help unweave it."

Olivia and I look at each other. We know of only one connection to Argentina, but without the identity of the real intended victim, it's pretty far afield. Or is it?

CHAPTER TWENTY-NINE

"The identity of the young lady has been verified by two sources based on the images we sent. Her name is Kwan Tan and she is a Korean national. She is twenty nine years old; born in Buenos Aires; was a bio-chemistry major at Berkeley and has a Ph.D. in public health from Beijing School of Medicine. Her father was the South Korean military attaché to a number of embassies, including Argentina until there was some sort of scandal concerning arms sales. I am asking Jung Kim to see if his resources can be more precise. She has no known connection with Kim Enterprises and her presence at the track is still a bit of a mystery. I hope Li Chin is able to glean something from the security video footage."

"What does Miss Tan do?" I ask.

"Thomas that is the so-called $64,000 question. After completing her post graduate studies, Kwan Tan basically disappeared. Her Korean passport shows she traveled extensively in South America, visiting the United States only once. She does not appear to have remained in any place for more than a week or so."

"This may sound a bit far fetched, but not as far as some of the things we have seen," Charles begins, "But can we check her travels against unexpected deaths of influential people at the same time and place?"

"Brilliant thought. A bit James Bond for my taste, but brilliant." Sir Bertram is standing in the doorway of the Hotel Bentley.

"Other than Sheriff Rosewood, you all know our friend, part time colleague and one of the most logical and devious minds around, the eccentric Sir Bertram Hollingsworth." Hans bows.

"Eccentric? Devious? In this group? Hardly. Be that as it may, our search for the elusive Miss Tan has yielded nothing concrete. No one can say with any degree of reliability that they saw her."

"Since we have so little to go on, maybe we should see if Kwan Tan's travels have a pattern. Is it a problem?" I am not averse to thinking like James Bond or should I say Ian Fleming?

"I have already entered the travel information from her passport into my computer. The data may be skewed if she has more than one passport. It may take a few minutes, but I am going to search major worldwide news services for deaths during Miss Tan's visits to those countries. It's all in the parameters I input. It is worth a try." Cecil fingers fly over his keyboard.

"The source of the type of VX has been narrowed somewhat. Although China is the country of origin, the specific product could have been sold to one of its allies, including North Korea and Iran or the VX may have found its way into the black market. VX is synthesized in relatively small quantities and each batch has certain markers which distinguishes it from another batch. The markers are relatively simple to isolate and we have engaged some very qualified folks to analyze the VX on Mr. Soo's hand. That's the good news. The bad news is that the batch markers are a closely guarded state secret and when we find the marker we may not be able to ascertain whether it was inventoried or sold to others. The use of VX is banned by the UN Security Council. But we see it or similar nerve agents being used time and time again without recourse. Although it is Saturday early afternoon here, it is early morning tomorrow in the Far East so I don't expect to receive the analysis for an hour or more. I am willing to keep a stiff upper lip and make things appear normal and get ready to race." Frederick has given us a lesson about the dark side, but the race shall go on. Nothing fazes these people.

Olivia returns as Pierre and Frederick, followed by Charles and Franco, who has replaced Cecil as pit crew, briskly walk over to their waiting steeds. "I spoke with Charlie, who is feeling a lot better. He drank too much coffee with too much sugar on an empty stomach. He does remember the woman who served the tea."

"Kwan Tan," Hans inserts.

"Charlie arrived at the garage a few minutes after 6 and Miss Tan was already there. She asked him if he wanted some tea. He said he was going to have coffee instead but thanked her. That's it. He didn't see her again. I searched for Mr. Soo's cup. There must have been a dozen in the trash. I pulled out the can liner, tied it and had one of Elias' deputies take it to Dr. Jacobson's office. I called him to look for a garbage delivery." Chief Detective Nederfield turns toward Elias and says, "I hope you don't mind the fact that I commandeered one of your officers. I specifically told him to put the trash bag in the trunk of the cruiser. It was getting a bit ripe."

Elias shook his head. "I can see why Josh promoted you. Initiative, intuition, and beauty."

"Here, here," Stanford adds. "Anyone want more pastry before I put them away?"

This army marches with a full stomach.

"Since it may be a few minutes before Cecil and his magic computer get search results, let us be a cheering section for my brother and Frederick." Mother Margaret has spoken, so it shall be done. We march off, in single file, behind her.

As much as I love watching vintage sports cars and vintage stock cars, vintage formula cars epitomize the period during which they raced. In a matter of only ten years, the cars morphed from fire burning front engine large displacement monsters to sleek rear engine nimble machines. During those ten years the careers of many of the prewar (World War II for those not old enough to remember) heroes ended while new chargers seized control. Hawthorne, Brabham, and Moss replaced Fangio, Ascari, and Farina.

The practice session is spirited but everyone is on their best behavior. I enjoy Frederick navigate the Connaught with precision while Pierre and Marshall Leventhal practically throw the Talbot Lago and Alfa through the turns. Alas, we have a murder to solve and not too many brilliant ways in which to do it.

Our march back to HQ is not as spirited as before because we are all deep in thought. I certainly hope that Cecil's search points us in the right direction or any direction for that matter. The master computer program designer and master chef have been left alone for almost forty minutes and the aroma of fresh garlic bread, pasta with tomato sauce and chicken sausage and braised eggplant fill Chez Bentley. We all look at each other and then at the feast which is laid out in front of us. "One must fuel the engine," Stanford observes.

"How do you guys solve any murders if you eat like this?" Palm Beach County Sheriff Rosewood asks.

"Don't ask!" Olivia and I answer together.

"While you all have been absorbing the ambiance of the race, Oscar and I have something to show you," Cecil announces.

"Oscar?"

"Thomas, please excuse our friend. If Sherlock Holmes has Watson, Cecil thought he should have a name for his computer . . . Oscar." Margaret's reply is said dead pan. Pardon my expression. Like everyone names their computer.

"This is a pictorial display of where our Miss Tan has been during the last year based on entries from her Korean passport. The red outline represents the countries she visited. I have asked a colleague to search for credit card charges Miss Tan may have made in each country so that the search area can be narrowed to specific cities or areas within each county. I have made a universal search to include people of some notoriety who died of some kind of coronary event in each outlined country during Miss Tan's visit. We already have over a dozen matches. Some may be coincidence; some may not be readily explicable. Hans, I hope you don't mind, but I called in a couple of favors so that we can access the decedents' medical records."

"Not at all. Why do these things always happen on weekends?" Hans shrugs.

"Speaking of medical records, Mr. Soo was healthy as a proverbial horse. Absolutely no medical issues. I spoke with Dr. Jacobson who confirmed the predeath status of Mr. Soo."

"Now what?" I hope I don't sound too impatient.

"Oh! We partake in the superb smelling meal that Stanford has prepared and wait for my sources." Cecil is so nonchalant. Big deal. It's only an inexplicable murder with no motives and no suspects and the entire G-7 will be here in a day and a half. Let's eat.

CHAPTER THIRTY

Because Hotel Bentley has been converted into a high tech crime laboratory, our luncheon is strictly buffet. Several tables are pulled from the side of the RV and a dozen folding chairs suddenly appear. "*Molto bene*," I shout.

"Don't talk with your mouth full. I'll call your mother." Olivia gives me a little punch in the arm.

Elias' cell rings. It sounds like war drums. He answers, grunts twice, pushes the off button and says, "Rachael may have a lead. She's coming over. I invited her to lunch. Is that okay Stanford?"

"Heavens! Another mouth to feed! What will I do?" His response brings laughter from everyone, except Elias, who will eventually figure out the dynamics of Team Bentley—maybe.

Deputy Silver jogs over from the Kim garage, barely breathing hard. Franco, omnipresent with beverages, hands her a bottle of water and beckons her to sit—next to him—not her brother or Olivia.

"We do not discuss business while eating. It ruins Stanford's hard work." Once again, Mother Margaret has spoken and all obey, although everyone seems to be eating a little faster.

"This is delicious," Rachael says after literally inhaling Stanford's offerings. "I never get to eat like this except when my mom cooks for us."

"Which is way too infrequent," Elias adds.

"I was under the impression that your family lives close by," I reflect.

"It is hard to explain. Our parents decided many years ago after I entered the Navy, that they were more comfortable living the old way. Their house is in the 'Glades about a mile from a paved road. My dad raises long horn Florida beef and mom grows her own produce. They have about forty acres of the best oranges in the state. They fish together and even go 'gator hunting. So if we want to see them, we need to plan a visit. Mike comes down about once every couple of months and we borrow an air boat from some friends and bring some hard to come by items for the house. Mostly books. It is why I was surprised you spoke to Elias in our native tongue. He told me it was a sign of respect, not disrespect as I had thought."

"*Cosapi ocheepeas.* Forgive us. We all speak many languages so that we can be understood and can also understand others. Please tell us what news you bring." Margaret Leiter is definitely the coolest person in the world.

"I met with a number of people who felt more comfortable speaking Korean. Since I don't exactly look like a round eye and my Korean has a little regional accent, most everyone thought I was from one of the islands. I told them my parents were from Jindo and my father was a fisherman. Everyone seemed fine with that except Lee Song, who is an employee of Kim Enterprises and has been here at the track since it was purchased. He asked me many questions about Korea which he assumed I couldn't answer. I knew where he was going but played along. His technique reflected someone trained in interrogation, but not extensively trained. I sent his finger prints, which I lifted from a cup from which he was drinking, and passport information, which I got from Jung Kim, to a former colleague now at NSA. Bingo. Mr. Song is not below the radar. In fact, his name surfaced just a couple of days ago when the Secret Service was comparing notes with several other agencies assigned to protect G-7 participants."

"Little sister, do me a favor. Here is a list of nine names including Sir Bertram, please call your contact and ask her to run these names by the person or persons with the highest security clearance that she trusts . . . immediately. I already know the answer but we must ask her some questions."

"Deputy Silver, may I suggest you ask your contact to call this number and ask the person who answers to call Hans Leiter. It will be a lot faster."

I can tell that Elias' sister has been in situations where you need to go with your gut. She excuses herself and walks to the far end of Hotel Bentley to use her cell. About a minute later, the deputy walks back, looking a little confused. My contact recognized the number and wanted to know how I got it. I begged her to simply place the call. She agreed. Hans' phone begins to ring.

"Howard, I need open access," Hans says. "Thanks. I'll explain later. Deputy Silver, we have a secure Zoom link inside. We need to call your contact in a minute. I am sorry about the cloak and dagger, but you know how it works."

"Thank you for taking me into your confidence."

"*Hink-lah-mas-tchay.* It is all well. Let us make that call. Cecil can you check on the mysterious Miss Tan?"

"Oh, I forgot to tell you. Kwan Tan was seen by several members of Kim's staff. She did not talk to anyone and seemed to stay near the refreshment. Basically . . . nothing. I asked Mr. Song if we could chat later. He was noncommittal."

"I'm going to talk with Jung about Mr. Song. Maybe Mr. Park as well," I will let the experts cut through the red tape of the spy world.

"I'll go with you and see how Li and Lu are enjoying the movies," Olivia adds.

"Olivia, can you call Dr. Jacobson and ask him to check for fingerprints on the cup which presumably contains the oleander? He can lift Mr. Soo's prints at his office and if another print is identifiable, it may very well be that of Miss Tan. I want to learn more about her background." Cecil is bothered by the possibility that Kwan Tan may have more than one passport which will complicate the matrix he is working on.

CHAPTER THIRTY-ONE

"I was expecting you," Jung Kim tells me. "I started to reflect upon the entire situation by removing myself as a potential victim. Based on what Mr. Leiter just told me about Miss Tan and Mr. Song, I do not see a connection between them or me. I know nothing of the young lady but have put together this file regarding Mr. Song. He was one of the youngest graduates from the Korean accelerated high school program in computer sciences. His father was a leading software engineer in the North and fled with young Lee almost twenty years ago. He was cleared by both national and internal security to work on some sensitive projects. However, out of an abundance of caution some of the data that Song the Elder accessed was intentionally wrong. We wanted to see if it migrated to the North. It did not, so he started to work on more high security projects. In the due diligence of the senior Mr. Song, the government examined any connections he might still have in North Korea. No family or financial connections were uncovered. He seemed to be a true intellectual unconcerned about politics and ideology. When Lee graduated from university, Kim Enterprises was happy to employ him. Lee Song was a bit of an introvert. He did not socialize with co-workers or attend any company events. I don't know about his views on anything outside the realm of his work. I don't picture him as a killer. The file says nothing else except that his work product was very good and he was afforded the opportunity to attend computer engineering conferences throughout the world. He worked on projects related to data gathering and analysis. His father suffered a major heart attack a little over a year ago and died. Lee became even more distant. The company offered him grief counseling, but he declined. When the decision was made to develop the performance center, Lee requested to be transferred from corporate headquarters to Florida to design the data collection. All the K-5 equipment you see is his brainchild."

"Your insight is helpful. I still want you to be watchful. Do you have a file on Mr. Park?"

"Funny you should mention that. I have been remiss by leaving a lot of the background checking to others. Since I knew his father, I assumed Mr. Park was what he appeared to be; a very conscientious young man. I have no reason to doubt that assessment except that his personnel file is missing and I can't find it in our data base. Needless to say, everything is backed up at corporate, but it is still very early in the morning and I will have to wait until an authorized supervisor is available . . . maybe four hours. Also I have asked about the father of the young lady. I have nothing on my computer, but it might be on a more sensitive server which I can't access until morning in Korea."

"I may be grasping at straws, but Lin Soo died of an apparent heart attack and Lee Song's father died of an apparent heart attack. Might there be a connection?"

"You are trying to connect the dots. I will also ask if there was a postmortem examination of Mr. Song the Elder.

Thomas, I am troubled that so many of my countrymen seem to be tangled in this web. I would feel better if this was less complicated given the time constraints, but in our business we seldom get what we want." Jung Kim shrugs.

"I am going back to Bentley headquarters to see if anything has turned up regarding either Song or Tan and will let you know."

"Thank you. Hans and Cecil have copied me on everything in and out so far, so I am staying up to date. I noticed Olivia is in with Li and Lu. Tedious work. The facial recognition software we are developing will allow you to submit an image and it can scan all data banks for any match. It's still a bit slow, but coming soon."

"From Kim Enterprises," I add.

"No doubt." We bow and I leave.

I slowly walk back to the RV. How am I going to make sure the venue will be secure? The repercussion of cancellation is unthinkable. I'm not even sure of the target and therefore coming up with a motive is futile. Is the target an individual or the event itself? Basically, other than putting a lot of wheels in motion, we don't have diddly squat. The lion's den awaits. I hope Olivia is having better luck. I continue trudging along, even more slowly than before.

"You look like you could use a cold Dr. Pepper," Stanford says when I finally reach Chez Bentley.

"Actually a single malt is more like it, but the Dr. Pepper sounds good," I reply.

"I take it old bean, that your meeting with Jung Kim yielded few pearls of wisdom," Sir Bertram adds.

"Sounds like a gross understatement." Cecil sounds a little too cheery.

"Lee Song sounds benign, but his father, who fled North Korea and ended up working for Kim, died last year of an apparent heart attack. Jung Kim is checking any medical records relating to Song the Elder and on Miss Tan's father. Also, Mr. Park's file seems to have disappeared although it is backed up at Kim Enterprises. Because of the time difference, we will have to wait a couple of hours."

"Cecil has encountered the time difference factor as well but has made progress on his matrix," Hans says.

"Did your Zoom conference yield anything about Lee Song?" I ask.

Margaret nods toward Deputy Silver.

"A little over a year ago Lee attended a conference of computer engineers in Brussels. He spent a great deal of time with two Russian software whiz kids. They were inseparable. That triggered Lee being put on a watch list by NSA. The three stayed in close e-contact. Shortly after the conference one of the young Russians was hired by a company with big time Kremlin contacts. The communications between them appears, on the surface, to be chatter about designing some kind of internet game. It may be for real or it may have been encrypted. Lee's transfer to Florida raised some security eyebrows, but nothing verifiable. He is simply a person NSA is watching, but having played their game for many years, probably everyone is a person of interest to someone. On a scale of 1-10, Lee Song is a 2 or 2.5. He is aloof and distant, but works hard and produces good results. All this is subject to finding out where Miss Tan was when his father had a heart attach."

"Well done Signorina Rachael." Franco is clearly infatuated.

"I hope I am not too late," Chief Detective Nederfield says entering the RV.

"Let me recap. We are awaiting information regarding Miss Tan's father. Also Mr. Park's personnel file and Mr. Song the Elder's medical records. Cecil is doing a data sweep to attempt to correlate Miss Tan's travels with suspicious heart attack deaths. Dr. Jacobson is trying to retrieve Miss Tan's fingerprints from the discarded cup from which Mr. Soo drank his fatal tea." Charles sees things through a lens and can keep us in focus.

"Is it fair to say that we are still on the false grid?" I add.

"Speaking of which, Pierre and I have another practice schedule in fifteen minutes . . . and we must continue to make everything seem normal." Frederick is correct but he is also being a bit facetious. I think the lack of a suspect or for that matter a victim is getting to everyone.

CHAPTER THIRTY-TWO

Once again practice goes off without a hitch. If we didn't have a murder to solve, I might feel really good. Olivia's cell phone rings.

"It's Sheila!" She whispers.

"Put her on speaker," I suggest.

"What's up?" Olivia asks.

"We have a perimeter issue. Possible breach. Can you meet me at Gate 4?"

"Sure. Was it a breach in or out?" I am curious.

"It's weird. Please hurry. I don't want to go to the next level of protocol response." TSA Director White is not a happy camper.

We hot foot it across the paddock. Sheila is standing with both Agent Forbes and Driver.

"We have what may be an intruder," She stammers.

"Sheila, please explain."

"Last night a man appeared at this gate for admission. He was stopped by one of Dan's guys and asked for ID. The man said *everyone knows me, I'm the owner*. A uniformed Palm Beach Deputy said that the man was indeed the owner of the track and that he had met him numerous times when he pulled extra duty time during races. The man told the agent that he had left his credentials in his office when he left on Wednesday but didn't return until last night because he had felt under the weather."

Olivia and I look at each other in total disbelief. "Charles Shaw! When did you find this out?"

"About fifteen minutes ago," Agent Driver replies. "I was going over the log of everyone who entered the track today against the approved list. Then I saw the page from yesterday. Charles Shaw had signed in using his driver's license as proof of identification at 7:17 pm."

"Before you ask, we have no record that he has left the track." Agent Forbes is shaking with anger.

"Well folks, I suggest you get Sheriff Rosewood on board and find the creep. Excuse me, former owner ASAP. This changes the dynamics in a big way." I am also angry. With all the security in place, things like his shouldn't happen. I never thought to keep a special lookout for Shaw because I thought he was in Korea. Shit!

Both agents, the TSA director, Chief Detective Nederfield and I all take out our phones and start dialing. We've added a wild card without having any idea of the motive or the intended victim.

"Jung, Charles Shaw is at the track." I pause. "I understand. Get as many of your people on the ground to find him."

"Olivia, we've got to let Team Bentley know. I am not sure what this all means, except that I have a bad feeling."

"Thomas, please take a deep breath. Shaw doesn't connect."

"Yes he does. I just haven't figured out how. Jung Kim said that Shaw was in Seoul on Wednesday. He is having Kim security check it out. He is asking his contacts to ascertain if Shaw has left Korea."

"Sheila?" Olivia shouts at the TSA director. "Can you check to see if Charles Shaw has entered the country in the last 72 hours? Probably Miami since there is a direct flight from Seoul."

"Great idea. I am going to get his passport picture distributed to everyone."

"No need!" Elias Rosewood approaches. "Dan Driver filled me in and I had my guys get his picture from his Florida driver's license. It's been texted to all my deputies and anyone on our law enforcement approved list."

Suddenly my cell phone vibrates. So does Olivia's and Sheila's. It's a color picture of former track owner, Charles Tilson Shaw. I'm impressed.

"Well done *Hi-e-pas eyaha* . . . Little Wolf.*"

"Quicker than sending a smoke signal." Sheriff Rosewood's laugh is infectious. "My offer about losing him in the 'Glades still stands."

"Let's find him first. I have a real bad feeling. Olivia and I are going over to Bentley headquarters."

We hustle over to the RV stopping briefly at the facilities. In addition to the Bentley Seven plus one, Sir Bertram, Deputy Silver, Dr. Jacobson, Sheriff Rosewood, Olivia, and yours truly, eight new faces appear on the jumbo screen.

"Chief Detective Olivia Nederfield, Deputy Thomas Ballard, Sheriff Elias Rosewood, may I introduce you to some of my associates at NSA, Interpol and the Defense Department. We have been chatting about Lee Song, and have concluded he is not a suspect in the murder of Mr. Soo, but nevertheless may be compromised regarding security issues. He will be excused from the property for the balance of the event and his continued employment at Kim Enterprises will be reviewed by the appropriate persons. We are focusing on Kwan Tan and her father, the latter of whom was incarcerated about a year ago after being found guilty of treason by the Korean courts. He was transferring information to both North Korea and China, neither realizing he was selling the same technology to each. He actually submitted himself to Korean authorities because he was afraid he was a target for assassination." Whenever Hans gives a briefing, it is succinct.

"Mr. Tan's fear was probably well-founded, but is there a connection to his transgressions and his daughter's activities?" I try to be equally on point

"This is where it gets interesting," Cecil begins. "While Miss Tan was studying in Beijing, she apparently fell in love with a young Chinese med student, who was actually a member of an elite military unit. By year's end, Miss Tan had been recruited to join his unit. Her skills in immunology made her a logical choice for a unique assignment: she became an assassin. Her weapon of choice was an oleander cocktail. Her beauty and language skills made her an ideal operative in South and Central America. I have compared her travels and unexplained cardiac deaths. They overlap too closely to be a coincidence. She is elusive and kills without any apparent empathy. Unless she has a cloak that allows her to disappear, she is still at the track."

"Since about half of the members of law enforcement in the world are here, I would like to ask two questions. Is that permissible Hans?"

"By all means," he replies.

"Has anyone identified the intended victim and why? Assume Kwan Tan is a hired gun; usually the person or entity has a target and a reason." I think I make sense.

"Simply said," a voice from the Zoom team says, "No! We have compared notes and no one presently at the track seems to be a potential target."

Elias addresses the monitor, "Inasmuch as this is in my jurisdiction, although Miss Tan seems to have created quite an international tempest in a teapot, I need to get everyone's opinion about the possibility that this was a dry run . . . a practice."

"The Sheriff brings up a very good point," Margaret Leiter begins. "Where the thread disappears is when we consider the presence of VX. Clearly, her connection with the Chinese military makes accessibility a non-issue. But it does not seem to be her *modus operendi*."

"Let me propose the following: the VX was intended to be a calling card and not the instrument of death. I saw many instances where a killer will leave evidence of their identity to intimidate survivors by showing they could kill at any time and at any place. Very common in Afghanistan," Deputy Silver postulates.

"Let me suggest that we close the Zoom conference and each of us spends an hour or two reviewing what has been said. We shall reconvene at 16:00 Eastern daylight time. The same link. Is that satisfactory?" Everyone assents.

CHAPTER THIRTY-THREE

The quiet is refreshing. At this point I am not sure where we are. It is imperative that we apprehend Kwan Tan, but if she is in fact an assassin for the People's Republic, getting any information from her will be impossible. I'm not sure what Li and Lu can add to the equation. Jung Kim's people might be able to shed some light on Mr. Park, but he isn't really a person of interest or is he? It is a bit off putting that his personnel file is missing, but that could be attributed to all the construction for the test center. I don't think there is much more to connect Kwan's father to anything, except possibly her radicalization. So, where does that leave us? Getting my hands around Charles Shaw's neck seems like a good idea, although I cannot fathom a connection. Maybe he hired Kwan Tan to kill Jung Kim because he bought the track, essentially putting Shaw out of a job and the prestige that went with it. That theory doesn't hold water though, because Jung didn't sack Shaw he kept him on the payroll. Maybe I am not being objective because of my dislike for Shaw as a human being.

"Knock! Knock! Thomas, you are talking to yourself." Olivia snaps me back to the here and now. "There are over one hundred deputies and agents searching for Tan and Shaw. Cecil and Charles with some weird hand held devices that I am told combine infra red heat profiling technology and a motion detector have joined Elias' sister. Cecil is creating a grid much like is used in underwater research, and plans to scan each sector for someone or maybe two someones who may be hiding."

I guess I feel better, but I'm not sure.

"All vintage cars are to be on the false grid in ten minutes for the final practice session," growls the PA system.

"Let's help Frederick and Pierre." At least that will take my mind off . . . whatever.

Franco and Stanford, who has been recruited as members of the pit crew, help the driver's climb into their cars. Stanford adjusts seat belts, while Franco quickly checks the tire pressure and fluids. He steps back and waves his arm in a circular motion. The peace and quiet is quickly shattered by the roar of their cars and two dozen others. These dynamic pages of history move slowly to the false grid and then onto the track to follow the pace car for a couple of warm-up laps. I notice that the speed is picking up each session and the cars are at speed when the Kim KIA pulls into the pits. The green flag is shown and off they go.

"I thought that the vintage cars were going to have three practice sessions. This looks like a race," I observe.

"The drivers voted to make the last session a race," Hans says. "I must say that the fraternity of vintage drivers is very democratic." He chuckles.

"Your fraternity is beginning to accept sorority members . . . finally," Margaret adds.

"It was a figure of speech my dear." Hans is on the defensive.

"*Mon amour*, I forgive you." Margaret gives Hans a kiss. Olivia gives me a kiss. Both Hans and I are speechless—a good thing.

"Let's watch our compatriots before we have to return to less pleasant matters," Hans finally says.

Frederick's British Racing Green Connaught and Marshall Leventhal's red and white Alfetta 159 are thundering down the back straight, followed closely by a silver Mercedes and a gorgeous red Ferrari 246. Close on their proverbial heels is Pierre's blue Talbot Lago T26C, a snow white Vanwall, and a V-12 Maserati 250F. The sounds and the smells are surreal. The race ends entirely too soon with a Ferrari 625 taking the checker flag. The cars return to the paddock. I am curious about the winning car. It did not take the lead until the next to last lap on a very well-executed pass of the other Ferrari and the Alfetta. Olivia sees me starring as the driver is extricated from the car. When the helmet is removed mountains of red hair cascade down to the driver's shoulders.

"She's the newest member of Team Ferrari; Carla Scotiani. She's only 22, but don't even think about it. Her father owns a hugely successful chain of boutiques and she always travels with a bodyguard." Olivia can be so mean. My interest was purely journalistic—more or less.

However, a motive popped into my head—kidnapping. However it is not consistent with murder and the Korean connection, but I think I should give Josh a heads up for next week.

Because Stanford was recruited to help with the cars, drinks are strictly self-serve from a cooler outside the RV. I guess we don't get any pastries.

We all gather for a Hans Leiter briefing. It will be short and to the point.

"I want to summarize where we are or more precisely where we aren't. Basically we have a suspect, Kwan Tan, who has so far avoided the long arm of the law. We also have two, so-called wild cards, Mr. Park and Mr. Shaw, neither of whom do I consider a serious candidate. Mr. Song is being detained for reasons not related to the murder but not altogether unrelated to the races. We have no motive except that Miss Tan seems to be a professional killer; but the identity of her target has eluded us. The presence of VX is an enigma. Anything to add?"

We are all silent—for a moment.

"What is the meaning of this? I protest. Do you know who I am?" Charles Shaw is screaming at two huge deputy sheriffs who are flanking him.

"Mr. Shaw, we know who you are and who you aren't," Elias Rosewood's voice is louder and deeper than usual. "Please shut up or I will put a gag into your mouth. I can add resisting a law enforcement officer to other pending charges."

"What charges? I have a perfect right to be here."

"Actually you don't." I resist putting my finger in his nose. "You lied to a Secret Service agent. That is a federal offense." I didn't know if it is or not, but I enjoy making Shaw sweat.

"Mr. Shaw, what were you doing here last night?" Hans' voice could melt butter.

"What business is it of yours?" That was not a good thing for Shaw to say.

"Sheriff Rosewood, I recall you have kin living in the Everglades, is that correct?" No one knows where Hans is going. "Since I have no business with Mr. Shaw, I thought he and I might take a ride out to the land of alligators and pythons for a chat about my business." I don't believe what I just heard.

"You may use one of our unmarked Explorers for your journey."

Shaw starts to scream, "You can't do this."

Agents Forbes and Driver walk over to the shrieking former track owner and flash their credentials. "Mr. Leiter is empowered by the highest authorities to do whatever is necessary and I mean whatever is necessary to keep this venue safe. Have a nice trip. Maybe we will have a conversation when you get back. Maybe not."

I am going to nominate FBI Agent Kent Forbes for an Academy Award. Eliot Ness couldn't have done a better job. I must admit Hans gets a best supporting nod. Charles Shaw deflates before our very eyes. He starts to shake and weep real tears.

"I didn't intend to hurt anyone. I put the stuff on the sink handle in the VIP bathroom. I didn't expect anyone to use it until Monday by which time I would have diligently discovered the substance and reported it. I would have been a hero for saving the life of some mucky muck."

Frederick, who is still in his driver's suit asks, "What stuff did you put on the sink handle and where did you get it?"

Shaw is completely encircled by a dozen really pissed off folks.

"I can't tell you. I promised my source."

"Sheriff, may I have the keys?" Hans is as cool as a cucumber.

"Mr. Leiter, may I come along?" Agent Forbes asks. "We have heard about your interrogation techniques at the Bureau and since this is a matter of national, actually international, security, I would love to observe."

"With pleasure. Sheriff Rosewood, may I borrow some tie wrap restraints?"

These two must have practiced this routine before. It's magnificent.

Shaw cracks like a broken egg. "I'll tell you everything."

"That's a relief. I wasn't sure I wanted to hold dinner until Hans and Agent Forbes returned." I noticed that Stanford didn't include Shaw as a returnee. These guys are so good.

"Deputies Lincoln and Tucker, I think we have this under control, but one never knows. Please bring my Explorer around in case we need it and then check in with Deputy Silver. I hope her treasure hunt is going well." Elias has obviously taken a bit of acting himself. I notice he didn't mention Kwan Tan by name.

CHAPTER THIRTY-FOUR

"Mr. Shaw, from the beginning if you please." I know Sir Bertram is on the edge of his seat.

"When I got to Korea there wasn't much to do. The project I was supposed to oversee was very behind schedule. I had a lot of free time on my hands. One of the things that struck me is how much the South Koreans obsessed about the North. People talked about the North Korean leader Kim Jong Un in hushed tones. The murder of his half-brother was continually referred to as an example of his ruthlessness and the necessity for vigilance. I started to go out at night, since I had no where to go in the morning. Well, one thing lead to another and I met some very unsavory chaps who were willing to sell me anything I wanted: women, drugs, guns, and even poison. At first I laughed it off, but as one week became four weeks, I wanted to return home. I wanted Kim Tire to acknowledge my worth and make me an equity owner of Gold Coast. It's what I've done for thirty years. It's who I am. I came up with a plan to put some deadly stuff in a place where it was dangerous, but discover it before anyone got hurt. I asked around and met a man who sold me a small jar of what he said was a deadly nerve poison. I paid him almost one-thousand dollars. That's it. I have no names."

I must admit, Shaw tells a great story. Unfortunately, it is totally believable. "What did you know about this weekend?" I ask.

"Initially, Monday was supposed to be a track day for the Sheriff's office, but then the project changed. I had heard that some very important people were going to attend exhibition races on Monday. I thought that would be the perfect time to execute my plan."

I wonder if the choice of the word *execute* was simply coincidental.

"Is there any poison left over?" Olivia tries to sound very understanding.

"Oh yes, most of it."

"And where is it?" Olivia sounds like a purring cat.

"Here in my pocket." He begins to reach into his blazer side pocket. Frederick grabs his wrist. Pierre who has already has put on surgical gloves, lifts out a small jar, like a cold crème jar and places it into the plastic bag Franco is holding. Elias marks the bag and gives it to Dr. Jacobson.

"I will run the test to confirm it is the same substance. I want to have the sink handle in the VIP bathroom sterilized."

"It's already being done," Margaret says. "As soon as Mr. Shaw told us how Mr. Soo came in contact with the toxin I texted Jung Kim. His brother-in-law and several security personnel familiar with handling VX will remove and bag any residue and clean all the surfaces. Mr. Soo may have touched another surface leaving the men's room."

Elias looks at me and slightly shakes his head.

"Don't ask," I whisper.

"Charles Tilson Shaw you are under arrest and charged with involuntary manslaughter in the death of Lin Soo. You have the right to remain silent. Anything you say can and will be used against you in a court of law. You have the right to an attorney. If you cannot afford an attorney, one will be provided for you. Do you understand?" Sheriff Rosewood is all business.

Shaw nods.

"Please indicate that you understand verbally."

"Yes, I understand." Shaw holds out his hands in front of him like you see in an old Bogey movie, but Elias cuffs him behind his back. Standard Operating Procedure.

One down, one to go. We have a suspect, but still don't have a motive or even the actual target. I am concerned we might never know. If Kwan Tan avoids being apprehended, we are definitely out of luck. If she is caught and decides to play hardball, we are still out of luck since the 'Glades routine is unlikely to work again.

"I have taken the liberty to postpone our Zoom conference two hours. I want to confirm that the VX, with which Mr. Soo came in contact, is the same as the material on the sink handle and more importantly the jar taken from Mr. Shaw." Hans is right. Shaw could be shooting blanks. I don't think so. He is too much of a wimp.

The two deputies, Lincoln and Tucker, escort Shaw to the waiting paddy wagon, which is actually a basic Crown Victoria.

"I will have him arraigned on Tuesday, so if any of you all have additional charges, let me know. I want him held without bail," Elias announces. "I can't believe that he could be so totally oblivious to the potential harm of VX."

"I think everyone needs a stiff drink, but I am going to postpone happy hour until after the Zoom conference," Stanford declares. "I think I'll make some hors d'oeuvres."

We all turn toward the RV's door. It sounds like a cat fight. Suddenly the door bursts open and Cecil enters. "We could use a little help. Deputy Silver has caught a wild beast who may need to be sedated."

Dr. Jacobson looks first at Hans and then at Sheriff Rosewood. He's got the pecking order correct. They both nod. He retrieves his little black bag and removes a vial of liquid and a syringe. Everyone moves aside but then closely follows him out of Chez Bentley. Charles is holding one end of a rope which is tied around a diminutive Asian women, who is kicking and screaming. The woman, Kwan Tan I presume, is being carried by the 6 foot tall Rachael Silver in a most undignified way.

"I brought you a present *Hi-e-pas eyaha,* big brother. All trussed up like daddy taught me." Deputy Silver unceremoniously dumps Kwan Tan onto the ground.

"You should have seen her," Charles sputters. "Unbelievable. Cecil got a heat reading under a trailer. As we approached, this woman rolls out and starts to runs. Deputy Silver, who is carrying a rope, lassoes the women and hog ties her in a matter of seconds. Just like *Wide World of Sports.* It was amazing. The deputy tried to talk to the women in Korean, but she spit at her. Deputy Silver picked up the woman and threw her over her shoulders and here we are. Unbelievable."

"Never mess with the Florida State junior's calf roping champion . . . three years in a row," a very proud brother says.

"Let me give her a little shot to calm her down. She's as mad as a hornet." Dr. Jacobson quickly administers the medicine.

"How long before Miss Tan is able to speak to us?" Hans asks.

"The dose was light, in part because of her size. I think within fifteen minutes."

"I suggest we secure her in a more conventional and ladylike manner," Mother Margaret says. "Do you have any leg shackles, Sheriff Rosewood. Handcuffs alone may not be able to hold her. And then we need to talk about jurisdiction. Interrogation techniques will have to be very sensitive."

"I think we should call Jung Kim and Li and Lu Chin." Olivia suggests.

"No need," a voice shouts from a speeding ATV. "We are here."

"That was fast," I quip.

"Remember Thomas, the entire track is under surveillance. Li saw the entire apprehension in real time and she came to get me. And here we are. Mrs. Leiter raises an excellent point about jurisdiction. I think there is enough evidence to hold Miss Tan for the murder of Mr. Soo. I assume her fingerprints are on the cup from which Mr. Soo drank, but regardless she is seen handing him the cup."

"In my analysis of her travels during the last year juxtaposed to unexplained deaths at the same time, a pattern is emerging. It will take some time to get medical records of the decedents. We may have to even exhume some bodies to ascertain whether there are traces of oleander. Motives will have to be discovered, if possible. I am not sure whether, without a confession, we will be able to connect the deaths to the Chinese government." Cecil is thorough.

"I can probably get a no bail order on a first degree murder charge, but if she is a Chinese agent, and they want her, she may be hard to hold indefinitely." Elias is cut short by a moan from the inert body of Kwan Tan. He quickly leaves the RV and returns a minute later with a full set of chains; ankle, waist and hand. Now we wait.

CHAPTER THIRTY-FIVE

"We have a dilemma facing us," Agent Forbes begins. "On the one hand, Miss Tan is subject to the Palm Beach County Sheriff's office. On the other hand, I can think of at least a half dozen federal crimes for which she should be interrogated."

"In all due respect, she is a Korean citizen and murdered a Korean citizen and we may have somewhat more effective ways of interrogation," Jung Kim says.

"Lest you forget, Miss Tan may be a person of interest in multiple murders in multiple jurisdictions and thus the matter should be turned over to Interpol." Sir Bertram brings up a good point.

"Before we start with the third degree, I have a few questions. Did Kwan Tan have anything on her person when you caught her?" I ask.

"She had nothing. I checked for suicide capsules. She has no identifying tattoos or birth marks. Nothing hidden anywhere on her person. Believe me, I have done this before and after seeing a male colleague almost killed by not properly searching a female suspect, I am thorough." Wow! Deputy Silver is one tough nut. "I have twice taken the oath to protect and defend our Constitution and I am not a proponent of physical interrogation, but I'm also not a proponent of assassinations. I would like about fifteen minutes with Miss Tan when she recovers . . . alone. Since I speak Korean, and as a woman I may be less threatening. She also knows that I can be tough and effective."

"I have mostly differed to others regarding matters of this nature, but I think that Deputy Silver is right. I want to add one minor suggestion; that I am also in attendance. I speak fluent Spanish, which is Miss Tan's first language and actually have some conversational Korean. As an older person, she may give me some additional respect." Margaret Leiter is calm and collected. I suspect that she has had more than a little experience in the art of interrogation and I know no one will pull the wool over her eyes."

"Having absolutely nothing to say about jurisdiction, I am inclined to give the ladies a chance," I suggest.

"I concur and offer my services. I speak Spanish as well, and have interrogated a lot of hard cases," Olivia offers.

"I'd throw my hat into the ring, but we're not sure Jung Kim wasn't the intended target and I might get a little personal," Li Chin adds.

"As most of you know we make decisions based upon the best information we have and upon concurrence of all of us. Is their any dissent to having Deputy Silver, Chief Detective Nederfield, and my wife spend a few heart to heart minutes with Miss Tan?" Hans is not really asking for a vote. He knows his team and we all agree.

"Quick *Miranda* question. Should she be read her rights?" Elias asks.

"The case will never get to trial," Agent Forbes answers.

"Gotcha," Sheriff Rosewood answers. "Rachael, do you want the keys to the restraints?"

"If we need them, we'll come and find you," She replies.

We all file out of the RV. I notice Deputy Silver and Olivia pick up Kwan Kim and place her in one of the large living room chairs.

"I'm going to check with the office. I sometimes forget that there is an international conference right down the street." Dan Driver has been mostly quiet.

"I've stocked up the cooler with water, juice, and Dr. Pepper for you Thomas," Stanford says.

"Pierre, let's put the babies to sleep for the night," Frederick suggests.

"Give me your driver's suits so that I can brush them out and hang them up," Franco dictates.

"Kent, care to join me in a quick walk about to make sure the troops are doing okay?" Elias asks. "I think Sheila needs some company."

I need to go use the facilities and then have a Dr. Pepper.

"Thomas," Olivia says from the open door on the RV, "I need you to go and find a bright yellow vintage car and crawl under the trailer. Between the two axles you should find a flat leather packet. Please bring it back as soon as you can." The door closes.

At 6'3" I can envision myself wiggling under a car trailer much less being able to retrieve anything. First, I've got to find a yellow race car. Most every one is putting away their cars for the evening, so I better hot foot it around the paddock. Fortunately I spot a bright canary yellow Cooper T 51 being pushed into the aforementioned trailer.

"Hi, I'm Thomas Ballard and . . ."

"The famous automobile writer?" A kid of about fourteen yells into the trailer. "Dad, come here and meet someone cool." I hope he wasn't putting his father down or me up.

"Nigel Goodwin here, a pleasure to meet you. We are great fans of your work." The man, sporting a neatly trimmed moustache and looking like Graham Hill extends his hand."

Before engaging in what I fear will be an extended conversation, I ask if his son will slide under their trailer and search for a leather packet. "It's rather important and I don't have time to explain. If you and your son will come over to the Team Bentley motor home in about an hour, I am sure I can explain everything."

Nigel gives me an inquisitive look. I do what I hate most. I show him my badge. "Roger, have a look for a leather case under the trailer between the axles. Thanks lad."

In under a minute Roger reappears with what appears to be an official document case. He hands it to his father who in turn hands it to me. It bears the logo of the People's Republic of China.

I thank the Goodwin's and quickly retreat. I am torn between examining the contents before I hand it over to Olivia. She outranks me and it might seem like I don't trust her. I knock on the door, which opens a crack. I hand her the packet.

"Do you want to place a bet?" Sir Bertram asks.

"On what?" I reply.

"The contents of that leather case."

"I have no idea except that it probably contains Kwan Tan's personal papers."

"I bet you one pound, no more Euros for us, that Miss Tan has a diplomatic passport." "Shit! I hadn't thought of that. You mean she'll claim diplomatic immunity?"

Sir Bertram nods. "But that wonderful status only applies to members of the law enforcement community. Hans and his team do not exactly fall into that category, which is why Margaret is in there. I think you could use a nip." He hands me a silver flask from which I take a sip. "Jung Kim's private stock. He sends me a case for Christmas."

"I didn't know you two knew each other." I am dumb founded.

"For years. I was his contact when he was stationed in the U.K."

The width and breadth of these folks' reach is unbelievable.

CHAPTER THIRTY-SIX

Within five minutes, the door to Hotel Bentley opens and Olivia hands me a document. She nods and closes the door. This is getting a little too complicated for my relatively simplistic mind. Sir Bertram looks over my shoulder at the document.

"Just as I suspected, a Chinese diplomatic passport, which now is in your possession. No passport, no immunity. This has all the markings of Margaret."

"Are you insinuating that my wife might do something irregular?" Instead of sounding indignant, Hans is smiling.

Kwan Tan is over her head.

Rachael Silver next appears at the door. "She wants to negotiate."

"With whom?" Hans asks.

"Someone who can guarantee her that she won't be extradited."

"Where is it she doesn't want to go?" Sir Bertram asks.

"I think she is afraid that if she returns to China she will be tortured and then killed. She muttered something about Bolivia, Ecuador, and Peru, as well. Her English language skills are perfect. Remember, she is a graduate of Berkeley.

Communication is not a problem. Kwan Tan was not too happy when she woke up from the sedative and started screaming about her diplomatic status, but Mrs. Leiter informed her that she had no proof that she was a member of the Chinese diplomatic corps. She said something about a passport, but we all shrugged."

"The team is pretty much assembled," Hans says as Pierre and Frederick return from putting away the race cars and Kent Forbes and Elias return from their stroll around the paddock.

"May I recap?" I ask. "I promise to keep it simple since that is the way I am thinking right now. Assume Kwan Tan confesses to the murder of Lin Soo, we need her to identify the primary target and motive. Sheriff Rosewood has a conviction and very long sentence here in Florida. I am not sure the Feds have the same open and shut case unless she admits to being an agent of the Chinese government. Here's the catch, killing Soo isn't really a Fed crime. If she killed others in foreign jurisdictions it becomes their problem with the help of Interpol." Sir Bertram nods. I guess I know how he fits into the picture. "Do you all have the authority to take extradition off the table?" I look at FBI Agent Forbes.

"If Elias gets what he needs for a murder charge, I can get the prerequisite authority."

"I see one problem," Sheriff Rosewood begins. "If Soo wasn't the intended victim, then I can't charge her with more, what we call second degree murder . . . nonpremeditated or alternatively voluntary manslaughter. Twenty years max. Maybe less if she has a sad story."

"I think that we should have a chat with the suspect. Maybe just Hans, Agent Forbes, Sheriff Rosewood, Thomas, Sir Bertram, and the three ladies." Margaret opens the door and we shuffle in. Kwan Tan is shackled head to foot. She kind of looks like a deer caught in bright headlights.

"Miss Tan, I have explained your precondition. As you can imagine, until we have the entire picture regarding your activities here and abroad, no promises can be made. Both Sheriff Rosewood on behalf of the state of Florida and FBI Agent Forbes are willing to explore a non-extradition arrangement. Sir Bertram, on behalf of Interpol, needs to have all the details about a number of incidents in which you may have participated, but he has no interest in prosecution if we all reach an agreement. Do you understand that everyone is going to have to act in good faith? That is the best I can do. I think that we have made it clear that there are other options, but we should explore the more traditional first."

"I understand and am willing to submit myself to your questions." Kwan Tan's voice is quite deep for a person of her diminutive size.

"Sheriff Rosewood, may I have the keys to the restraints?" Margaret calmly retorts.

"I am obligated to recite your rights before we begin," Elias says and reads Kwan Tan her so-called *Miranda* rights. "Do you understand?"

"Yes, I do."

"Because of the seriousness of the situation, I must keep you only in handcuffs if you assure me you will cooperate and make no efforts to escape."

"Monsieur Rosewood, may I suggest that Miss Tan be placed in a pair of our handcuffs which we have designed. They are made of titanium, can only be opened by a remote electronic device and have an embedded GPS tracking chip." Pierre hands Elias a pair of very high tech looking, black, hand restraints and the remote.

"I will cooperate. Thank you for your courtesies. I am tired of running and want you to see the entire picture before you judge me, proverbially speaking." Kwan Tan is very resigned to her circumstances.

Sheriff Rosewood fastens Kwan Tan's wrists.

Everyone finds a place to sit. This is going to be an interesting story. As far as I am concerned, I am applying the old grain of salt adage

"Before we begin, I would like to ask Miss Tan several questions, the answers to which will affect my continued participation." Kent Forbes is going for the jugular. "Have you ever committed a crime, other than the events surrounding Mr. Soo's death, in the United States?"

"Other than smoking a little weed while in college on a ski trip to Colorado, I have not broken any laws in the United States." Kwan's answer seems forthright.

"Have you ever committed a crime upon a United States citizen or against property of the United States whether within the United States or abroad."

"No."

"Those are my jurisdictional threshold questions," FBI agent says.

"May I ?" Sir Bertram asks no one in particular. "Have you contributed in anyway to the death of any individual?"

"Yes, but it is not what you think. May I explain?"

"I think we should let Miss Tan tell us in detail her experiences at Berkeley and beyond," Margaret suggests in a way that says *this is what we are going to do*.

"I was awarded a full scholarship to Berkeley to study bio chemistry and did quite well. I was accepted at several doctoral programs, but the financial aid offered was not sufficient to allow me to attend. I decided to work for a small bio tech start-up in Silicon Valley. The pay was good, but the stock options held a lot more promise since our trials were going well. Three years ago my father, who was the military attaché at the Korean embassy in Buenos Aires, told me that I had been awarded a full stipend for the Ph.D. program in public health from Beijing School of Medicine. It was a two-year program since school is in session eleven months a year. I would have preferred attending an American program, but beggars can't be choosers. At the same time my father told me he had a new Mercedes. Members of the embassy do not make the kind of money needed to buy a Mercedes, so I assumed it was used, maybe a hand me down from the ambassador. I didn't think much more about it and started to prepare for my studies. I received an email from my father wishing me good luck and giving me several contact numbers in Beijing if I needed anything. He also attached a picture of himself and a very attractive young non-Korean Asian woman standing in front of a brand new Mercedes convertible. I was both confused and angry. My mother had been dead for five years so my father dating did not bother me, but the woman was as young as I . . . and Chinese. I said nothing. May I have a glass of water?"

"Certainly," Stanford answers. "We also have fruit drinks and soft drinks."

"Water is fine, thank you."

Stanford hands her a bottle of water with a straw. "I thought it might be easier to drink.

"Please continue Miss Tan," Margaret Leiter suggests.

"The program was very intense. The courses in English, but some of the science was different." "How can science be different," I ask.

"The approach to research in disease prevention is vastly diverse. Drugs are brought to market much earlier than here. Third phase trials are unheard of. The product is simply introduced into a control group . . . no volunteers. In any event I was really unhappy until I met a med student, who paid a lot of attention to me. He took me places students don't get to visit and basically wined and dined me. Then he told me that he was a member of the Chinese intelligence community and wanted my help. Of course, I refused until he said that my father had been providing the People's Republic with Korean military secrets and was being paid handsomely. If the source of those secrets was disclosed to the government of South Korea, mostly likely my father would be tried for treason and executed."

"What kind of help did they want?" Olivia asks

"Basically they wanted me to assassinate enemies of the government. Assassinate is not a fair word because all of the people identified had been found guilty of crimes and sentenced to death. However most had fled to South America. What could I do? I traveled to South America, met and ingratiated myself to those for whom death warrants had been signed, and was able to replicate heart attacks using a very powerful species of oleander."

"How did you dispense the oleander?" Frederick inquires.

"Always in a liquid. Sometime tea and sometime alcohol. It was always fatal."

"Do you have the names of your victims?" Sir Bertram is looking for loose ends.

"Yes and all the paperwork provided me, including dates and dosages. I fulfilled eight death sentences. I was promised that my father would be isolated from further involvement and my obligation was deemed completed. That was before it was discovered that my father had been selling the same secrets to both the Chinese and the North Korean military. There was nothing I could do. It turned out that the Korean ambassador to Argentina became aware of my father's duplicity and reported his actions to Korean intelligence instead of giving him a chance to redeem himself or disappear. Confronted with the option of facing the Chinese or North Koreans, he opted to confess to Korean officials. He was able to negotiate with them to waive a death sentence and serve twenty years in a low security prison in exchange for providing some misinformation."

"Miss Tan, we have corroborated most of what you have told us, so we believe it is true. However, the gravamen of the current situation, the death of Lin Soo, remains unexplained." Hans sounds a little impatient.

"Let me make this simple," Deputy Silver begins, "Who was your intended victim?"

"Lin Soo, of course. It was personal. He and my father had been friends for years. He served as a permanent member of the Korean delegation to Argentina during all the time my father was military attaché. He discovered the dissemination of secrets. He never gave my father a chance to explain."

"Other than greed, was there an explanation?" I think my question is apropos.

Suddenly Kwan Tan begins to weep. Her façade cracks. "I simply couldn't believe that he would betray our country. There had to be an explanation. I asked him after he was arrested. He did not answer. I assumed there must be a reason. Something honorable. Maybe it was a plan to trick the Chinese or North Koreans and that what he told them was a ruse. My anger became so obsessive that I began following Lin Soo and when he came to the United States, I followed.

I knew he was a friend of Jung Kim's and so when I learned about his attendance here, I planned to poison him. I thought that pretending I was a hostess, a guise I had used before, would work. I devised serving traditional tea and honey as a cover. The tea I offered was untainted until Lin Soo accepted my offer. I crushed a small capsule against the lip of the cup and the powdered oleander dissolved in the hot tea. I did not know that there would be a pretend shooting nor that someone would use VX. It was a perfect plan."

"Almost perfect," Elias Rosewood says. "It appears that the charge against you will have to be increased to murder in the first degree, but I will opposed the death sentence because it was an act of passion, although you have shown yourself to be a rather cold blooded killer, I guess that a jury would only hear that you were fulfilling a legal sentence upon a foreign national in a foreign territory."

"Miss Tan, please provide me with the names of those to whom you administered coriander and the writs of execution issued by the People's Republic. If they are in order, Interpol has no interest in this case." Sir Bertram immediately identifies the quagmire.

"You will find everything in the leather pouch including all my computer passwords."

"Agent Forbes, do you have any comment?" Hans asks.

"This appears to be a local matter." Agent Driver nods his assent.

"Sheriff Rosewood, I think you need to revert to your restraints for the prisoner to be transported." Elias nods and retrieves the handcuffs which he affixes behind Kwan Tan's back, returning the cool high tech cuffs to Margaret.

Everyone is silent. Rachael Silver places her hand under Kwan's elbow and guides her out of the RV. We all follow.

The prisoner is placed in the waiting patrol car. Without lights or sirens, it proceeds toward the gate.

"Sheila," Olivia says into her cell, "Palm Beach County cruiser is approaching. It is cleared to exit. Crisis averted. Come by for a well-deserved drink and I'll fill you in."

"I am exhausted," I offer.

"It is the proverbial wind being let out of your sails. Thomas, the event is secure," Hans contributes.

"Right!" I somewhat understand Kwan Tan's acquiescence to the threats from the Chinese government, but redirecting blame from her father to Lin Soo, who simply did the right thing, is not acceptable, and I refuse to feel bad for the consequences which may befall her. I intend to compartmentalize these sordid events and enjoy the balance of the week and upcoming racing.

"Thomas, are you okay?" Olivia asks.

"Yup. I officially proclaim happy hour!" Everyone looks relieved and ready to move on.

"I'll need about ten minutes," Stanford shouts. "Everyone wash up. Franco, can you lend me a hand?"

"Con piacere. With pleasure."

Also by D.G. Stern
The Adventures of Upton Charles—Dog Detective

Disappearing Diamonds
Something Fishy
Winter Wonderland
Lost Loot
Ship Shape
Tip Top
Picture Perfect
Time Tale

And coming soon
Missing Map
Super Scary
Look into the Mirror
Iced Tea ... Warm Corpse

Other books by D.G. Stern
25 Days of a Tropical Christmas
The Loneliest Tree
Sophie the Skunk
Francis the Firehouse Mouse
Hot Tea . . . Cold Case
There's Always Tomorrow
Stabbing Along the Straightaway
Chaos at the Concours
Panic at the Pits

Visit us on the web at:
www.neptunepress.org